Y0-BXQ-890

So Dies the Dreamer

Also by Ursula Curtiss

THE FACE OF THE TIGER

THE STAIRWAY

WIDOW'S WEB

THE DEADLY CLIMATE

THE IRON COBWEB

THE NOONDAY DEVIL

THE SECOND SICKLE

VOICE OUT OF DARKNESS

So Dies the Dreamer

Ursula Curtiss

DODD, MEAD & COMPANY
NEW YORK

Library of Congress Catalog Card Number: 60–8442
Printed in the United States of America

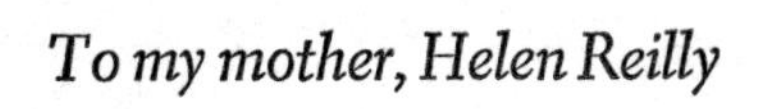

To my mother, Helen Reilly

So Dies the Dreamer

i

EVEN NOW, three months later, Sarah Trafton could not rid her mind of the idea that it all went back to the mink farm. Or to the pheasants, in some way, although that was even more tenuous.

It had to go back to something, it had to have started somewhere. Except in the cruelest jokes, sane, happy, newly-married men like Charles Trafton did not jump from twelfth-floor windows. On the other hand, had he been sane, at the end?

Sarah had one pinpoint to proceed from, although she had dug at it so savagely and often that it was now more like an open wound: the night the trouble had first showed itself.

It was in the small Bermuda hotel where they had spent their honeymoon. She was asleep and dreaming; she had waked, heart pounding with shock, to the frightful sound that seemed even then to lodge itself in her body, like a pain that promised to come again and again. In a woman it would have been a scream; in Charles it was a groan that mounted and quickened and grew, so that only Sarah's sharp cry and wild reaching for the lamp stopped it from turning into a shriek.

The room was instantly, abnormally quiet, as though they had both stopped breathing. The bedside lamp had overturned under Sarah's frantic hand, and shone with foolish tranquillity on the floor. The travelling clock Charles's aunt had given them said three-thirty. In the other bed, Charles had turned his head inquiringly on the pillow; his narrow intelligent face was calm, his eyes bright. He said, "Hello," in as alert and amiable a voice as though it were noon, and then, with a faint frown, "What was I doing? Snoring? Making a racket?"

It was impossible that he didn't know; his heart must be pounding, if anything, harder than hers. Sarah said shakily, "You were being torn limb from limb. Or else you dreamed you were just getting to the church again. Charles, I *never* heard such a noise."

Charles rolled over on his back—because the light bothered his eyes, or because he didn't want her to see his face? "Cheese?" he asked reflectively of the ceiling. "That last cordial? The way to a man's nightmares is through his stomach. Sorry, darling, I won't do it again."

Nightmare. She had had nightmares herself, she had heard other people have them, at home, at college, in the apartment she had shared with another girl before her marriage. But this . . .

She went into the bathroom for a drink of water, and lit a cigarette on the way. Her panic had not so much subsided as hidden itself; across her mind, put out of it instantly, flashed a recently-read item in a newspaper, about natives in—Africa? India?—who were dying in numbers, apparently of fright, in their sleep.

Voodoo, said Sarah comfortingly to herself. Bone-pointing.

They had then been married five days.

Neither of them made any reference to that peculiar interval in the night the next day, or in the days that followed. Charles looked sunny and unworried, and except for a vague unease before she went to sleep, Sarah firmly forgot the whole thing. They swam a great deal, drank at odd hours, and dined elaborately, trying to outdo each other in their definitions of the wine.

"A small wine," Sarah would say gravely, and Charles, after a great deal of sipping and frowning and head-cocking: "I would go further, I would say almost a tiny wine." His glass lifted, his head went back. "In fact, an invisible wine," said Sarah.

The night before they left for home, it happened again: the riven groans, coming closer and louder, mounting to an infinitely beseeching pitch, the stopping just in time. This time Sarah said directly, "Charles, what were you dreaming about just now?"

"You know what it is?" countered Charles, with an air of worry erased. "It's all this peculiar food, very rich for a country boy, and all this swimming. My system thinks it's changed hands."

Sarah did not smile. She hadn't knocked over the lamp this time, and she could see the betraying dampness of his forehead above the clear triumphant gaze. "If you have nightmares, you must have some idea of what they're about. Everybody does. They're falling, or trapped in a burning building, or— Charles, you must know."

"But I don't know," said Charles in a mimicking voice,

and looked at her face and sat instantly upright. "Sarah—sweet—I'm sorry, I didn't mean to—"

"Don't be silly." She smiled at him stiffly and consciously, as she might have smiled at some effortful stranger. "It's just that I'm worried, a little. It can't be awfully good for anybody to keep dreaming like that, and it's not, if you follow me, very flattering."

"It has nothing to do with you," said Charles sharply, and, after a moment's total silence, "You're right. Tell you what, I'll have a check-up when we get home. It'll ease your mind if nothing else."

But he didn't. When they were settled in the apartment in New York's East Thirties, he said, "Yes. Tomorrow, remind me," and Sarah reminded him to the point of naggery, but he always slipped out of any positive appointment.

The nightmares—call them that although it was like calling a hurricane windy—went on, and settled into a dreadful pattern. If he drank a great deal, he slept the night through, but was accordingly edgy in the morning. Three cocktails did it at first, and then three cocktails and wine with dinner; at length a nightcap had to be added, and then increased to two.

On the nights when he didn't drink, Sarah went shrinkingly to sleep, knowing that she would be waked, and how. No matter how steeled she was, the impact was always just as frightful. It was like standing outside a torture chamber, knowing what must be going on inside, powerless to help.

And Charles changed in other ways.

Sarah had never analyzed her reasons for marrying him, but they were there. By the time she was twenty-two, both her parents were dead. Her only brother had been killed in Korea, her sister was married and living in San Francisco. Inevitably, and with the help of friends in the Connecticut town where she had grown up, she had gone to New York to look for a job.

It was a typist's job to begin with, and then a secretary's, and then a secretary's in an advertising agency. With some talent and a great deal of luck, she had ended up in the copy department. She was well-bred and quick and attractive, an ornament to trot out for clients, and another two years went by before she realized the sterility of this small particular world.

The women she knew were dedicatedly smart, witty, beautifully dressed, intensely clever, and knifingly ambitious. The men she knew were witty, charming, helpful, and married, seldom less than twice. Some of them took her out for cocktails after work, waving a negligent hand at the train their wives would be meeting in the suburbs, before she realized quite what was going on.

Through a fabrics account, she met Charles Trafton. He wasn't the client but a friend of the client's, and he came from somewhere on Boston's South Shore. He was almost apologetically good-looking: narrow lively face, fairish hair, spare nonchalant height. He didn't speak the sparkling advertising liturgy, and to Sarah, reacting violently from an attachment to an art director who had kept his third wife and four children under wraps, he was a good deed in a naughty world. He was sunny, he was open, he didn't need to bolster himself up with a lot of fifty-dollar-an-hour complexes. He worked in the New York office of his late uncle's Boston publishing house, and he had no plans for advancement over the prone bodies of his colleagues.

He said the second time he took her out to dinner, "Do you like pheasants?"

"I've only had pheasant once, but then it was— What are you laughing at?"

It took him some time to recover. "I meant live ones, you know, walking around. Tame. I have an aunt who keeps them, and I'd like you to meet her."

So tame himself, or rather, trusting, so blessedly open; all she had to do was say, with becoming modesty, that she would like to meet his aunt, too. Sarah gazed at him through her lashes, realized with irritation that it was a trick she had picked up from her group head, and looked at him honestly.

"What pretty eyes you have," said Charles Trafton dreamily. "Green. Someone with blue eyes started that business about the green-eyed monster."

It was really settled then and there, although another five weeks went by before they became engaged. Sarah and Charles drove up to Massachusetts that Saturday to see his aunt, a startling sixtyish woman who looked like a retired actress but was really the widow of a railroad executive. Her name was Bess Gideon, and the wooden legend at the foot of the driveway said "Pheasant Pharm," which Sarah loyally did not flinch at.

There were other people in the old, expensively restored farmhouse. Bess's son, Hunter Gideon, was perhaps forty, tall, brusque-faced, sun-reddened; give him a mustache, thought Sarah, and he would look like a television lawman of the early West. By contrast, Bess's nephew Milo was an owl, plump, secretive, with an air of malicious wisdom. His wife, Evelyn, was dismayingly unsecretive; before ten minutes had gone by she had commenced with energy on a list of her—could it really be sixty-four?—separate allergies.

Sarah, composing her features to the proper blend of fascination and sympathy, gazed back into the busy protuberant blue eyes and had a moment's faltering. It was true that she was not marrying any of these people, not the lawman nor the owl nor this sandy woman who talked as though her life depended on it, but they were Charles's background, the only family he had, and he must have been conditioned by them to some extent. Would he expect her to be like Evelyn, for instance, or his rather daunting aunt; would he expect . . . ?

At that all-important moment Charles caught her eye, gave her a very small rueful smile, and turned back to his conversation with Hunter.

And there were the pheasants. Sarah, wrapped up in Charles, bothered by his relatives, trying to split herself in two to absorb both factions, was still dazzled by the beautiful, surprisingly calm birds who walked the immaculately-kept wire pens in the angle behind the attached barn. They were black and silver, flame-red and green and cream, bronze and yellow and blue—and then, when the sun struck them, an indescribable range of colors in-between.

While Sarah watched, a dun-brown bird walked into a shaft of light and became a precise pattern of shimmering blue-eyeleted copper. She was afraid to move, for fear of alarming this exquisite creature, but Charles bent carelessly, plucked a handful of grass blades, and held them to the wire. The pheasant came forward at a delicate questing walk, tipped its head to give Sarah a curious round-eyed glance, and took the grass hungrily.

"They love dandelion greens," Charles said, "and they will go anywhere for raisins or boiled potatoes. Look at them, they expect some now."

It was August, and the late-afternoon hour when the low sun, in spite of its richness, recaptures the absolute clarity of early morning. The shadows on the clipped grass were deep and exact, the pines that formed a windbreak beyond the far pens seemed to show forth every needle. The air was faintly fragrant, the lacing of bird-calls so peaceful that it was a part of the silence.

Charles was watching the pheasants; briefly, Sarah watched Charles. His face was quiet with pleasure, clear, uncomplicated. The particular segment of New York she lived in, the barbed brilliance, the smiling, deadly, daily competition, had never seemed more impossible, nor farther away.

"Time for a drink," said Charles, almost reluctantly. "I'm sorry about Evelyn. Once she's run through all her allergies she'll go off and fasten on somebody else. In a way, they're the only distinction she has. The thing to do is get your mind firmly on something else, she won't notice anyway. I've composed a lot of letters in my head listening to Evelyn."

Sarah, still spellbound with peace, said that she didn't mind Evelyn at all. They were turning to go back into the house through the stable and barn when a woman's deep clear voice behind them said, "Charles?"

Even before she turned, Sarah's mind registered the impression that this was not a cousinish voice, nor an auntish one. Kate Clemence was obviously neither. She was a tall woman, as tall as Charles, with ragged black hair, cut that way out of carelessness or immense guile, black-lashed gray eyes, and an air of unbreakable calm. She wore dungarees and a man's white shirt, open at the throat, and if she had walked down Madison Avenue just as she was she would have been snapped up instantly by scouts for something or other. Sarah hated her with a hearty intuitive hatred before she said so much as another word.

The Clemences—Kate and her brother—lived, Charles told Sarah in the course of introductions, in the house just visible through the pines. (How nice for them, thought Sarah, faintly shocked at her own spite.) Kate was wonderful with birds, it was a touch she had—(Oh, better and better) —and had often helped Bess Gideon doctor an ailing cock, or set traps for an occasional marauding mink from the farm nearby.

Sarah and Kate exchanged smiles of practised sincerity, and Sarah wandered tactfully away, given an excuse by the sudden appearance of a small, feather-hatted, pantaletted black hen. It was, Charles told her later, one of the Japanese Silkies, bantams kept to hatch the pheasant eggs. Pheasants would not hatch their own young in captivity, while the Silkies would sit on anything, or, if there weren't anything, on nothing, folding their wings dedicatedly on bare boards. A deep square of sod had to be placed under the nest to provide the dampness necessary for hatching pheasant eggs, but once the chicks had emerged the Silkie would treat them like the one of her own in the same hatch, although hers did not have to be taught how to eat as the pheasant chicks did.

The hen at Sarah's feet seemed expectant and a little cross; when she knelt and held out her hand it pecked at her palm and gave her an injured look. Behind her, perhaps ten feet away, Kate Clemence said murmuringly to Charles, "They've found out who the dead woman on the mink farm was—did Bess tell you?"

"No."

Kate's voice dropped cautiously on a name. Charles was not as cautious; Sarah, vainly offering grass to the black hen, heard him say in an oddly fumbling way, "Not the Miss Braceway . . . not the nurse—?"

Kate Clemence must have nodded. "You know that little hut out there, at the edge of the woods? The police think some man . . ."

Sarah strolled farther away on that; the compassionate note in the other woman's voice was not for her ears. The nurse—what echo did that bring up? That Charles's stepmother, of whom he had been very fond, had died several months ago of pneumonia. Here in this house, in fact. Charles had stayed here toward the end, and he would naturally have gotten to know the nurse.

Found out who she was. That suggested something singularly unpleasant, some unthinkable effort to prevent identification . . . "Here," said Sarah summarily to the black hen. "Pheasants like dandelion greens, why don't you?"

Some man. She must have been young, then, or youngish. Above her, Charles said in an almost normal voice, "That's Midnight. She was raised in the house, and she's very spoiled. Let's go in and get that drink, shall we?"

His face looked strained when Sarah rose. Kate Clemence had gone—having thrown her bombshell, Sarah thought angrily, having wiped out Charles's quiet contentment. He said abruptly, "That was rather unpleasant. The nurse who took care of my stepmother has turned up dead, in—" he nodded vaguely at pine-hidden distance "—a field up the road. She was fifty if she was a day, sensible, immensely competent—I can't imagine . . ."

He broke off, shaking his head. Sarah, released from a

shadow burden, said simply, "How ghastly . . . Someone in the woods, do you suppose?"

Charles shook his head again, blankly, and they went through the stable, converted to pheasant pens, and into the barn, hung with old harnesses, bridles, horseshoes. A blue-painted door opened onto the passageway that led into the kitchen; when Charles opened it a busy pattern of voices filtered through. His face lit; he said to Sarah, "Harry Brendan was going to try and come tonight. I hope he's here. He's the one person I'm most anxious for you to meet."

. . . Harry Brendan.

ii

For Sarah, the same instinct that had recognized Kate Clemence was on the alert for Harry Brendan. She knew that she was going to marry Charles, and something in her resented this unseen man whose approval Charles wanted, and to whom he unconsciously deferred. Buttonholed by the allergic Evelyn, aware of Milo's pseudo-scholarly malice on the fringe of the conversation, she watched the door.

A number of people came in, were introduced to Sarah, and drifted about Bess Gideon's long, vivid living room with the two sweeping pheasant feathers poised with an air of significance over the doorway. There was an old bull's-eye mirror over the fireplace, its gilt framed inside with a circle of black, and after a while Sarah watched all their expertly reduced figures in that. It was something of a shock to meet the reflected gaze of a man who, from his entrenchment in a corner and the drink in his hand, had obviously been there for some time.

He was Harry Brendan, Sarah knew that at once. He must have come in very quietly, with someone else, and something about the steady quality of his gaze suggested that he had been observing Sarah at his leisure. She glanced away without hurry, feeling her face grow hot for no reason, and then, disastrously, she glanced back.

As he must have known she would; his waiting eyes made it like a door re-opened, an appointment kept. Later she knew it for one of those freakish exchanges between strangers, the second of perfect contact that can happen in a crowded restaurant or a milling railroad station; at the moment she was conscious only of resentment and an obscure feeling of disloyalty to Charles.

By the time Charles introduced them, the moment was gone and she could wonder that it had ever existed. Harry Brendan had lost his magic; he was only Charles's friend, a few years older than Charles, darker, leaner, fractionally less tall. Sarah smiled and said how nice it was to meet him; Harry Brendan smiled back and said did she know Skitter Schofield, who was the account executive on Supersheen?

Later, Charles said anxiously, "How did you like Harry? Of course you didn't really get a chance to talk to him."

"He seemed very nice," said Sarah.

That was the first of several weekends at the farm. She and Charles were married in October. Harry Brendan was to have been best man, but at the last moment he sent word that he had come down with something indefinable and a man named Tom Proctor, whom Sarah had never seen before and never saw again, took his place.

She could have coped with or at least understood Charles's drinking. What left her weaponless was the inner and deeper change in him, the darkening of the sunniness she had fallen in love with, the sharp new cynicism. It was a little indecent, as though she had married one man and was now living with another.

She said one day in November, with the quiet of desperation, "Charles, if you'd only tell me."

"Tell you what?" asked Charles with the edge of his fourth cocktail. "The time? A story?"

She must keep her temper at all costs. "What's worrying you. What wakes you up at night—and me too—with those horrible nightmares."

Charles stared meditatively into his drink and then up at her. He said with distinctness, "Do you know, I think you're the last person I'd tell?"

"Thank you," said Sarah, white, but in the pause it took her to get that out, Charles was on his feet, holding her, saying inarticulately over her head, "Sarah, I didn't mean— I don't know what made me— Look, I'll go see what's-his-name, on the first floor, tomorrow. You'll see, all I need is Vitamin P or something. He'll make a new man of me and we'll have to get married again. Sarah?"

She managed to smile at him; she told herself that she had forgotten the clear considered rejection of a moment ago.

And he did go to see the doctor this time, and came back with a small bottle of white tablets which he displayed with an air of triumph. "Snakeroot," he said cheerfully. "I take one before retiring, and when I start to hiss and dart my tongue at people I discontinue the prescription."

Sarah was not quite satisfied; when he had gone to his office she called the doctor. He told her, after some preliminary confusion with the file of a man who had gallstones, that her husband was in very good shape physically, pulse a little fast, blood pressure a little high, perhaps, but those were quite usual reactions in people who were worried about a visit to the doctor. For the trouble in sleeping, he had prescribed a mild sedative which ought to establish a sleep pattern—

"But the nightmares," said Sarah. "If they haven't a physical cause . . ."

"Nightmares?" said the doctor blankly.

Charles took his pills, or said he took them, and for the first few nights he did not cry out but thrashed about a good deal and took gaspingly deep breaths which were almost as frightening to listen to. It was as though his private demon had been muzzled and might break free in some new revengeful form.

There was a brief surcease the week before Thanksgiving. Sarah was walking down Fifth Avenue in the late, cold afternoon when she paused, looked again at the woman waiting for a taxi, and said incredulously, "Kate!"

Kate Clemence, oddly diminished in tweeds, with pearls at her ears and a gray felt flowerpot that she kept giving vain little pushes to, seemed equally surprised to see Sarah. She said she was in town to do some shopping, was staying at a friend's apartment, and hadn't gotten in touch with Sarah and Charles because they wouldn't want to be bothered by callers so soon. Sarah looked wonderful, and she needn't ask how Charles was.

Nevertheless her large calm gaze did ask, and Sarah said instinctively, "Oh—fine, but he'll never forgive me if I let you get away. You'll have dinner with us tonight, won't you, Kate?"

She was already casting ahead to the difficulties of that,

the tenseness in Charles, the too-many cocktails, when Kate Clemence said firmly, with thanks, that she couldn't. She had undertaken to meet her friend's visiting aunt at Grand Central, and dinner had been all planned somewhere, but she had time for a cup of tea if Sarah had.

Over the tea, Kate said, "Are you coming up for Thanksgiving? Bess had an idea you might, and I know she's looking forward."

"We'd love to," said Sarah, "but unfortunately . . ."

She launched into a long effortful lie, because that was something else new in Charles—his withdrawal from people and places he had always been fond of. Only a week ago, when he had come home from his office paler and tenser than usual, Sarah had suggested a weekend at the farm. Instinct made her hesitant when he was in this mood, but she was totally unprepared for his brilliant, gradually-focussing stare, the mocking twist of his mouth. "Now that's a thought. So," said Charles, dropping ice cubes into a glass and splashing bourbon, "is this. Here's how." And now it was the drink that held his stare. "*Here's how* . . ."

He didn't even want to see Harry Brendan. Under other circumstances it might have been flattering; as things were, it added one more depth to Sarah's worry.

"Oh, what a shame," said Kate sympathetically when the tale of business commitments was finished, but as her clear gaze never altered by a hair it was impossible to know whether she believed the lie or not. "By the way, tell Charles, in case Bess hasn't written yet, that they've caught the man who killed the nurse. He'd been fired from the mink farm a few days before, and apparently he'd been holed up in a hut on the property, drinking steadily, ever since. Heaven knows what he was planning, but they think he mistook the woman for somebody else."

Sarah told Charles that night. His gaze turned intense, first on her and then on the rug. "Peck, was it?"

"Kate didn't mention his name, just that he'd worked on the mink farm. She said you'd know."

"Peck," repeated Charles with the barest of sighs. "My God, poor Peck. He's been panhandling and odd-jobbing around the town for years, just because he's got a face he can't help. I suppose that kind of thing comes to a head some day—" He rubbed his eyes with a kind of relieved violence. The news seemed to have sobered him, although he had never mentioned the nurse's death to Sarah after that first day at the pheasant pens. He had a weak highball after dinner, took his tablet without the usual mockery, and slept all night without stirring.

So that was it. Something to do with Charles's deep fondness for his stepmother, and shock at the tragedy that had overtaken the nurse who had seen her through her final illness—Sarah was too relieved to try and reason it out beyond that.

The mood of peace lasted for two days.

On a snowy late-November night, the apartment deceptively tranquil and flowery with light, Sarah said quietly, "Charles, you seem to be able to stand this, but I can't. I know you won't tell me what it's all about, but will you see a psychiatrist?"

It was the last thing she had ever expected to say to the clear open man she had married, and Charles found it equally bitter. He didn't turn from the window where he stood staring down into the street; he said with a short angry laugh, "Get thee to a nuttery?"

"Oh, stop that," said Sarah, holding her voice and her despair on a perilously short leash. "Go talk to some competent man—that's what they're there for—for my sake if not for your own. I can't—"

The leash snapped suddenly under weeks of strain and she turned away, blinded by tears. She would have liked to walk out of the apartment, coatless, hatless, into the bitter wind and snow; she would have gotten some release from inflicting on her body a little of the battering that her mind was taking. But Charles said her name beseechingly, and when she turned back and looked at his face she would not have dared to go out now and leave him alone.

Neither of them mentioned a psychiatrist again. In the week that followed, salvation came from an unexpected source. Charles's publishing house was putting on a publicity campaign for a new book of pseudo-spiritual counsel—"A collapsible halo comes with it," said Charles—and he stayed late at his office, working. Exhaustion did what neither the sedative nor the liquor had been able to do; that and the new, if temporary, preoccupation. He slept for fewer hours, but he slept soundly. He went to Chicago to see the author and came back looking more cheerful than he had in days.

Sarah was accordingly alone a good deal. She fell into the habit of having her own dinner early and then, because Charles would not be home until nine o'clock or so, going out to an early movie or any exhibition that was open or just for a walk.

She had come to the shocking realization, on that last bad evening, that Charles was and always had been weak; that his air of cloudless serenity was the retreat of a man who does not allow himself to become involved. His openness was, to some extent, emptiness.

She didn't say it to herself in so many words, she didn't even consciously think it. And who could define the exact point where love turned into fondness and concern? But her nerves knew about it even if she didn't, and played random tricks on her. Once she thought she saw Harry Brendan coming out of a theater lobby; another time she would have sworn that the tall man turning impatiently away from a piece of sculpture in an Indian exhibit was Hunter Gideon. Milo's portentous, down-sliding, horn-rimmed glasses occurred on a number of faces glimpsed from the corner of her eye, but when she turned her head the face was always a stranger's.

And, of course, if any of them had been in New York, he would have gotten in touch with Charles, and Charles would have told her.

Sarah went back to the apartment at a little after nine on a night early in December, and there were men waiting there to tell her that Charles was dead.

iii

Harry Brendan came at once; so did Bess and Hunter and, a tactful day later, Kate Clemence. All of them urged their offices kindly on Sarah, but, apart from the throat-constricting task of asking Harry to pick out clothes for Charles, she handled everything herself, steadily, numbly, not thinking backward or ahead but only of the immediate detail to be settled.

The usual expressions of sympathy were a little awkward, because it was established—although the short newspaper account said "fell or jumped"—that Charles Trafton had committed suicide.

In the way that funerals can, it had at times the air of a very important party. There was the stir and bustle, the inspection of the liquor supply, the disposition of the flowers that came to the apartment—"I think there, don't you, or is that table too small? Perhaps if we put the roses . . ." It wasn't any diminution of grief but a steadying factor, a needed crutch.

Bess Gideon, her handsome face becomingly haggard

under her short gray curls, took businesslike charge of everybody's hats and gloves, for which Sarah was grateful in a dimly amused way. "Kate, give Sarah your hat. It's frightful on you and it'll give her a veil without looking like weepers. Perhaps you ought to try Sarah's on first, but I'm quite sure . . . I've two extra pairs of gloves here, and I think long ones, with that coat—"

Kate Clemence slept at the apartment the night before the funeral, apparently on Harry Brendan's instructions. He said to Sarah flatly, "You can't be alone," and when she answered savagely, "I'd rather be," he looked down the length of the room to where Bess Gideon was frowning over a note she was writing, Hunter was mixing a nightcap for all of them, Kate Clemence was swinging one long narrow foot and making quiet suggestions to Bess.

"Now you would be," said Harry Brendan. "Later— I've been through this, and I know."

And he was right. When he left a little later, and Bess and Hunter went back to their hotel, and Kate Clemence said to Sarah, "I'm going to run a bath for you. No, stay where you are," the fact of Charles's death broke upon her overwhelmingly.

Water rushed in the bathroom, but otherwise the apartment was remorselessly quiet. No one commenting on flowers, no more telegrams to send and none arriving, no one to call; everything that should be done had been done. Now was the time to realize that Charles had come home—at 8:05 P.M., and how official that sounded—and not found Sarah there and, probably, paced up and down for a while before he did what must have been in his mind for some time. Walked to the window in the dining alcove at the end of the living room, opened it, perhaps stood there briefly wondering what kind of welcome he would find in the icy killing space, and put himself—there was no other word for it—out.

He had grasped at the curtain very fleetingly; there was a break in the blue loose-woven cloth and a corresponding thread of blue under one of his fingernails. It wasn't, said one of the large well-intentioned men Sarah had talked to, an uncommon gesture.

Apart from that, everything had been as meticulously neat as Charles himself. The elevator man remembered that Mr. Trafton had looked a little funny, coming up. He had had a drink; the bottle and glass were still on top of the bookcase in the alcove when the police entered the apartment, and upon the routine analysis the glass contained nothing but bourbon.

Sarah said that yes, her husband had been showing signs of emotional strain. His immediate superior at the publishing house said that Charles had looked "nervy," and that he had advised him more than once to take a rest or see a doctor. The doctor in the building, looking at the whole affair with hindsight, said shrewdly that while Mr. Trafton had exhibited only a normal nervousness at the time of his only consultation, it was entirely possible that . . . and so forth; while he wasn't a psychiatrist he had seen similar cases . . . and so on.

There had been no note, but then, thought Sarah somewhere in the reaches of the night, what could Charles have said?

It was all over with surprising speed; the ritual that took so long in the preparing ended with a back-to-work briskness. The limousine that had been driven with such hushed solemnity ripped back into the city at seventy miles an hour. Bess Gideon said as though it were a line from a play, "Sarah dear, come to us. Or is it too soon?" and marred the effect somewhat by asking for the long gloves which nobody had worn.

Kate Clemence looked white and ill, which didn't surprise Sarah; she had known the moment she saw her that the other woman was in love with Charles. Hunter Gideon, restlessly anxious to be gone, took Sarah's hand with a gentleness that astonished her and gave her one of the fierce looks he couldn't help. "Take my advice and get yourself out of here. A hotel, anyplace."

And then they were gone. Harry Brendan had not even bothered to say goodbye. Sarah, widowed after six weeks of marriage, went back to the wilting flowers, the clock-ticking silence, the letdown, and found Harry sitting on her living room couch, turning over the pages of a magazine.

He would have used Charles's key, of course. She couldn't remember giving it to him, but there were a lot of things that had escaped her in the past few days. He stood up at once, saying briskly, "Do you want to change your hat or wash your face or anything before we go to lunch?"

"But I'm—"

"What," said Harry with an air of detached interest, "were you planning on having for lunch? That skinless lemon? A few ice cubes? I had a look at your icebox, which I hope you don't mind, and that's it."

He took over, sweepingly, impersonally, that day and the next, and got Sarah through the first few dreadful hours. He knew restaurants she had never heard of before, and his quiet and faintly morose air brought waiters running. He was good for her, because although he did not attempt to

shut her out from reality—he asked her point-blank about Charles's insurance—he cushioned it a little. It was like being escorted by a male nurse, or so Sarah thought until the proprietress of a small Village restaurant sent them, with a knowing twinkle, a cordial on the house.

It was peculiarly embarrassing. The waiter cocked his head smilingly and glanced from Sarah to Harry, the proprietress waited beamingly in the distance. Harry lifted his glass to Sarah after the smallest pause. "They know me here," he said.

But what had been effortless became instantly a burden. Harry saw Sarah into the apartment house and said, gazing at the faded oriental rug in the lobby, that he would be going up to Boston the next day. Was there anything further he could do, any messages he could take?

Sarah said no, and thanked him for everything. There was no one to watch them except a white marble bust which bore a suspicious resemblance to the renting agent, but they were both too conscious, and not quite formal enough, to even touch hands. The elevator came, and the last she saw of Harry Brendan for almost three months was his quiet unsmiling face and his hand lifted in salute.

They had spent a good part of the past forty-eight hours together, but at no time, beyond the briefest shrug and head-shake, had they touched upon what could have driven Charles to suicide. Harry seemed to be waiting for Sarah, and to Sarah it would have been bitter beyond words to try and extract from Charles's friend the burden Charles had chosen to die with rather than to share it with his wife. She might be able to do it later; she couldn't do it now. It would make the whole thing too—pitiable, like opening a lifesaving letter that had come too late.

But she wondered, through the days and the nights.

She kept the apartment, because she didn't know what else to do. Somebody, probably Bess Gideon, had tactfully put away Charles's things, and Sarah was queerly relieved that the framed snapshot of him that she had kept on her dressing table had been removed, although she could not have done it herself.

Could Kate Clemence have . . . ? Sarah put that out of her mind at once, along with the realization, new for some reason, that Kate must hate her, must have found it very difficult even to be near her.

After a week or two, in desperation, she started working again. Not at the agency; although she might have gotten her job back, she flinched from the cheerful teasing inquiries of people who wouldn't have seen the brief obituary. On a deeper level, she flinched from being whispered about as the brand-new widow of a suicide; eyebrows couldn't help being raised, lightly cruel theories being advanced. From time to time, to pad out her income, she had done free-lance copy for a lingerie house, and it meant no more contact than telephone calls and envelopes exchanged by mail or messenger. They were delighted to hear from her, and they sent her a number of lavish garments to start extolling at once.

It didn't get her out of the apartment, but it put up a merciful smoke-screen in her mind. Instead of Charles's pleading eyes, she stared at satin rosettes, insets of lace, cunning panels of elastic that would theoretically make nymphs out of nonagenarians. She would think desperately, "*Why?* . . ." and then her gaze would fall on a scrawl from the manufacturer: "Positively can't ride up."

When Charles's will was probated, she owned the pheasant farm.

Sarah had never realized that it was his. It must have been left by his father to his stepmother, and gone to Charles upon her death. When she thought of all the people housed there—Bess and Hunter, Evelyn and Milo—and their absorption in the place, the disposition of it seemed uncomfortable and unfair. Sarah wrote a brief and awkward note in response to Bess Gideon's long formal letter proposing to buy the farm: she had never considered its coming to her, wouldn't know what to do with the pheasants or the bantams, and couldn't things go on as they were for the time being at least?

No indeed, Bess Gideon wrote back, delicately hostile. They could none of them consider taking advantage of Sarah's generosity. If she would name a price, they would try to meet it. In case their own resources fell short, Kate Clemence was interested in investing money in it.

Kate Clemence, who walked about so calmly and superbly in her man's white shirt and dungarees, who had "often helped Bess doctor an ailing cock," who had been in love with Charles. It was right, it was eminently proper. Kate had known all those people for years and would know exactly what to do with the pheasants and the bantams. Sarah ripped a nightgown ad from her typewriter and wrote back, shortly and unequivocally, that she didn't want to sell the farm.

And there, apparently, it rested. Bess Gideon did not write again. The days somehow turned themselves into next-days, and certainly no writer for Daintease had ever put more passionate energy into the account.

But at night, unavoidably, Sarah had to walk through the dining alcove into the kitchen. That end of the room changed every night after dark, in spite of the fact that she had bought new fabric for the window, a rough red sailcloth Charles had never seen, and didn't bear the imprint of his last unavailing impulse. But the view was the same: the high windows opposite, the topplingly foreshortened ground-floor apartments, the hats with shoes striking out from under them as people passed on the pavement below.

Sarah paused there one night with a curious forcing of muscles, and made herself press her forehead against the cold glass pane. She did not dare open the window to step deeper into Charles's mind. Grief had long since gone, to be replaced by pity and a piercing wonder. How could he . . . *why* had he?

She had thought uncertainty was frightful, but under that, unadmitted, was the notion that the truth might not be possible to live with. Suppose, for instance, that an understanding word or glance, an interview with someone, would have drawn Charles back from that killing plunge? Suppose she had had the strength to pretend that those frightful sounds had not waked and tormented her, that they were a passing thing, and dismissed them accordingly; might Charles then had dismissed the cause of them, too?

She found out early in January that she could not have hit upon anything more ironic.

iv

It was a woman who called her. Even before the emphasized "Mrs. Charles Trafton?" and the more distant, "I have Mrs. Trafton for you," Sarah's ear had identified her as a trained intermediary. Someone from the publishing house? Something to do about Charles's estate?

It turned out to be a Dr. Jonas Vollmer, a psychiatrist whom Charles had consulted on three separate visits.

Sarah took the receiver away from her ear and looked astoundedly at it as though she expected to see Dr. Vollmer, bearded and meditative, peering out of it. She put the receiver back, and said tentatively, "I wasn't aware that my husband had seen a psychiatrist. Are you sure you have the right . . . ?"

He sounded taken aback himself. "Sarah Trafton, nee—here we are—Fitzpatrick? Married to Charles Andrew Trafton on October nineteenth of last year in St. Anselm's Church? Let me see, first visit on November—"

Sarah lost the date, and the two subsequent dates, in the somehow stunning surprise that Charles, whom she had urged to see a psychiatrist, had done so without telling her.

Perhaps he had wanted to come to her with results, and three visits, she knew from a number of people at the agency, were hardly sufficient for recounting the people who had slighted you in infancy. Or was this something about a bill, overlooked in the general confusion?

She said, "Yes, I see," still trying to recover herself. "I don't know whether you're aware that my husband . . . ?"

It was so hard to say, but he was expertly ahead of her. "Yes, Mrs. Trafton. Very sad. Very," there was a rustling of papers, "unnecessary, I'm sure. I only learned of this development on my return from an extended trip abroad, and I may say that on the basis of what I learned from Mr. Trafton I am—dismayed."

There was a profound pause. Sarah pondered with amazement the word "development"; surely, even to a student of the mind, it was more than that? Dr. Vollmer said, "It occurred to me that you might care to see me," and Sarah said, "I certainly would, Doctor. When?"

He quoted her address at her, said that he lived only a few blocks north, and that if she would have a few minutes free at six o'clock he would call on her then. Sarah hung up, her stomach fluttering, her nerves in a tangle. Did psychiatrists make it a habit to drop around and visit the—what was the word—relict? She had never had any experience of them, but she didn't think so. And the measured gravity, the caution . . . of course, it was hardly a feather in a psychiatrist's cap to have a new patient commit suicide.

Nervously, she tidied up the apartment. He would undoubtedly think it meaningful that she was writing copy for feminine undergarments after her husband's death, so she covered her typewriter, folded the wings of the table, and pushed it into a corner. There was probably something equally significant in putting freesias in a low silver gravy bowl, but she refused to move that. Lastly, she looked at herself, six pounds lighter, face so much paler and thinner that only her peaked dark brows and green gaze stood out of it. Of course, lipstick; she put that on and regained a little self-possession.

Would he have a drink, or, if offered liquor, think that that she had lured Charles into alcoholism? If she offered him tea, would he think she had driven Charles into alcoholism by default? If she offered him nothing, would he find her hostile, negative, not out-going, or whatever the current phrases were?

At the back of her mind Sarah had a comforting notion that this was all nonsense and he would not be difficult at all. She was wrong. He was.

In the time it took to say, "Mrs. Trafton. How do you do?" and "It's kind of you to come, Doctor," they had arrived at a mutual dislike. Sarah's came in part, and unjustly, from the man's appearance: the square measuring face, very white, the full button mouth, the humorless examination he gave her and then, with a slow deliberate turn of his head, the apartment. It seemed quite possible that his slim leather case held scales and a blindfold.

Probably he hadn't liked her face either, or was it simply an automatic prejudging? Pet breeders looked darkly upon children, pediatricians looked darkly upon parents. A psychiatrist would be almost bound to view with disapproval the widow of a patient.

If it had only been that. After a few introductory skirmishes, Vollmer told Sarah the basis of her husband's nightmares.

Charles had been afraid of her, literally and physically

afraid of her. In his recurrent dream he stood on a height, and Sarah, behind him, threw something blue and muffling over his head and began to push him toward the edge.

(And she had said to Charles on that last night in Bermuda, "But you must know what they're about. Everybody does. They're falling, or . . ." Might as well remember it all, his sweat-damp forehead, the bitter mimicry of his voice, his instant, shaken apology . . .)

Blindly, as she was apt to do in moments of stress, Sarah lit the wrong end of a filter cigarette and took a lung-scorching breath of it while Vollmer watched with clinical interest. When she could speak again she said fairly steadily, "I'm afraid I don't quite . . . It seems a little late in the day to explain that I loved my husband. I was also," she knew this was a mistake, but an incredulous hurt and a growing anger at Vollmer's calm precise black-and-white face drove her on, "fond of my father. Not unhealthily, if that's possible any more, but I certainly have no hidden urges to push adult males over cliffs." Except perhaps right now. "Or are you telling me that my husband was insane?"

She was instantly aware of having fallen into a trap. Vollmer said with satisfaction, "Insanity is a term which we now . . ." and Sarah rebelliously stopped listening. Her heart still pounded with shock; she felt that it must be shaking her visibly. She emerged to hear the pedantic voice saying, "—has its cause. Perhaps an incident in childhood, involving someone whom he subconsciously indentified with you, or his feeling for you. Perhaps a phrase or a reference from you yourself, which at the time . . ."

And all at once Sarah knew.

She had to listen to a great deal more before she managed to get them both on their feet and edging toward the door:

Charles's relationship with his stepmother—this was something a psychiatrist could really get his teeth into; his preoccupation with the beautiful and useless pheasants, his concern over the death of the nurse. "Perhaps something quite interesting there," said Vollmer musingly. "The failure—you follow me?—of the nurse to save the stepmother's life. A feeling of bitterness and even of vengeance on Mr. Trafton's part. Her death at someone else's hands following upon that . . ."

He looked at Sarah's withdrawn, unlistening face. He said, "Perhaps you wonder why I was anxious to get in touch with you, Mrs. Trafton. I felt it only fair, as of course it was my duty, as soon as I learned of the sad event, to let the police know that Mr. Trafton had been a patient of mine."

And why, thought Sarah, crystally alert again. She said, "Of course. Very thoughtful of you, Doctor, and very conscientious."

They were sworn enemies now.

"I thought you might best be—prepared," said Vollmer.

He occupied the surface of Sarah's mind only briefly after he had gone. No profession could guarantee its every member; there were bad dentists, negligent doctors, unscrupulous lawyers. She had just been visited by a man who was, she suspected, so much in love with the trappings of the profession as to obscure its purpose.

Vollmer didn't matter, nor the fact that, at nearly seven o'clock, she would have liked a drink and ought to be doing something about her dinner. Nothing mattered except the astounding thing that she had remembered.

It had taken place on the last weekend she spent at the farm before her marriage. A friend of Evelyn's had dropped in with five children who demanded refreshments in loud whispers, fought in doorways, teased Milo's pet crow and then, having inspected the lawns and pheasants and let clouds of flies into the house, began to demand to go home. Their mother sat there like an untidy rock. Charles and Sarah, with the abstracted air of people who were only slipping into the next room for an ashtray, fled.

The afternoon was gray and windy. Although it was only late September, and asters and zinnias still blew about in the borders, a few crisp nights had begun to gild the huge hickory tree in the field where they stopped for a cigarette. Sarah knew that the mink farm lay somewhere off in the distance on their right; out of a reluctance to return to the house so soon she nodded at a rise behind trees to the left. "Where does that go?"

"Well, we used to call it a cliff," said Charles, smiling, "and then it shrank to a bluff and now I think it's only a hill. Let's have a look."

The wind came up sharply when they emerged from the band of trees, spinning Sarah's hair against her face and blowing it into her eyes. Charles went up the mossy rock-strewn slope ahead of her with a stick poised; he had remembered stepping into a nest of blacksnakes here. Sarah felt in her pocket for a scarf which she began to put over her hair as she walked, and just as Charles turned to say something to her the wind whipped the silk square from her fingers and pinned it against his face.

His head went back instinctively, and the sudden motion threw him off balance. Sarah ran up, half-blinded herself by her hair, and caught at his arm so suddenly that they both staggered.

And that was all there was to it: a freakish current of air, a second of lost footing. Charles wanted to know, laughing, if she thought this was Lover's Leap, and Sarah got her hair tied down and looked somewhat shakenly over the edge. It was still a very respectable bluff, the leafy drop perhaps twenty-five feet to what, from a glimpse of rocks at the bottom, had once been a brook bed.

To anyone who fell, it wouldn't have presented any mortal danger. But to someone who was pushed with force and went outward, with no tough wiry bushes to check his plunge . . .

After a while, as stiff and strange to her own living room as though she had actually been to Preston and back, Sarah went out to the kitchen, opened the refrigerator, and gazed blankly at the lamb chops she had, as usual, forgotten to thaw. She had tried not to slip into the canned-soup routine of women suddenly left alone, but somehow she often ended up that way. Tonight the alternative was two eggs and a stranded-looking piece of cheddar cheese. She shredded the cheese for omelette and made herself a drink while she waited for the pan to heat.

Memory did not let go cleanly. There were other wisps of that gray afternoon: Evelyn running to the field to meet them, her face red with effort and irritation, crying distractedly, "Sarah, that dreadful child insists that you have her bracelet."

Charles said, "You don't mean to say they're still here!" and Sarah, remembering, drew out the bracelet she had pocketed somewhat briskly after having it tobogganed from the crown of her head into her lap several dozen times.

"They're out in the car; they're going," panted Evelyn over her shoulder, and ran off.

The pheasants were still agitated by the unaccustomed

invasion of pounding feet, bursts of giggling, and sticks thrust curiously into their pens. Some had taken refuge in piled fir boughs, others were pacing about with short darting steps, heads tipped vigilantly. A Silver cock, black crest erect above his proud red-felt face, gave loud grunting cries of rage while Bess Gideon tried to soothe him with pieces of tomato.

When they went inside, Milo was vainly trying to cheer up his depressed crow.

Sarah was secretly relieved that Hunter Gideon was not there for dinner; she always had a nervous notion that he might bark a military command at her without warning, which she would obey before she thought. She and Charles went for a drive later, ending up at a roadhouse for a drink, and Charles said, smiling at her across the table, "This time next week . . ."

Whatever he might have thought later, whatever curious twist his mind had taken, he had not thought then that Sarah had tried to push him over the bluff; he had not even remembered the incident. Sarah was sure of that. Something had nudged it into his mind after they were married, distorted it, given it credence.

Or some other secret thing had gnawed away at Charles until his reason was actually clouded, and he turned blindly on the nearest scapegoat.

How appalling to think that she had lived with Charles and never known that this was going on; how wincing the memory of waking him, hand on his shoulder—*her* hand—from that racking dream of the height, the something blue over his eyes, the gathering push.

Had her scarf been blue? It must have been.

So had the thread of curtain caught under Charles's fingernail.

Sarah felt abruptly and physically sick. She forced herself to eat a little of the omelette which had burned on the bottom, and do the few dishes. She retreated to the living room with her coffee and picked up her face-down book, hating Dr. Vollmer for having led her to this depth, almost hating Charles, the stranger to whom she had betrayed herself so unknowingly.

The next morning, considerately out of uniform, Lieutenant Welk paid her a visit.

V

Sarah remembered the lieutenant from that otherwise lost night when Charles had died: a compact, light-footed man with the most interested gaze she had ever seen. Even while his voice said soothingly, "Now, Mrs. Trafton . . ." his fascinated glance had been examining the ceiling, the few pictures on the walls, the cut of her suit, the titles in the nearest bookcase.

What was it Vollmer had said as he left? "I thought you might best be prepared."

Sarah had not slept very much and looked it. She greeted Lieutenant Welk with a flicker of nervousness and, as her own third cup stood noticeably on the table in front of the couch, offered him coffee. Welk interrupted a piercing study of her narcissus shoots to say yes, if it wasn't a nuisance. She was on her way out to the kitchen when the telephone rang.

It was unfortunate that it should have been Mr. Eigel, of Daintease, who needed some rush copy for a trade paper ad and insisted upon having his girdle notes read back to him. Sarah tried circumspection, had to abandon it, and wondered rather wildly what the lieutenant was making of all this. She turned her head a little and saw him studying an old hunting print with such concentration that he would certainly have been able to pick up any of those choleric-looking gentlemen, pink coats or not, if he should find them in the neighborhood.

She was able to hang up at last. Lieutenant Welk, supplied with his coffee, tore himself from Sarah's book, which he had picked up and commenced reading, and said mildly that they had had a visit from a Dr. Vollmer, Mr. Trafton's psychiatrist.

Sarah said nothing. Her heart thudded.

"Interesting," said the lieutenant, "and, in a way, satisfactory from our point of view." He gave her an apologetic glance and got up for another look at the hunting print—to memorize the fox this time? "When a man like Mr. Trafton—in good health, with a good job, nice income, new wife—commits suicide, we presume temporarily unsound mind. That is on your own testimony, and his doctor's, and his office's. It's neater to have it officially endorsed."

What was he saying? That Charles's unsound state of mind had not been temporary at all? Or that a conviction that his wife might be plotting his death was enough to drive any man to temporary insanity?

Sarah said steadily, "It came as a complete surprise to me. I had urged my husband to go to a psychiatrist, but he never told me that he had."

Welk picked up his hat and gazed into it, apparently riveted by the size he must have been wearing for years. "How are you feeling now, Mrs. Trafton? Things settled down a bit?"

That girdle ad. "I'm doing a little work again, copywriting, which seems to help."

"Take a while to get over a shock like that. To come home from a movie and find—" Welk shook his head in mute sympathy, and Sarah could almost have laughed at the transparency of the trap.

"Not a movie, Lieutenant, a walk."

"Oh, a walk, was it?" He was imperturbably interested. "I thought policemen were the only people left in New York who walked." They both smiled at this droll observation. "Well, thanks very much, Mrs. Trafton."

"Thank you, Lieutenant."

Sarah did not immediately look it in the face. She had a fourth cup of coffee, one over her self-imposed limit, and went grimly to work on the trade ad. Mr. Eigel insisted on saying, not very originally, that Daintease girdled the world, but he might possibly be lured away from that by some reference to outer space. The phrase sounded a little unfortunate in connection with girdles, and she sat for a while staring absently at her notes. Formula from Venus? Diana Wore a Daintease . . . ?

. . . And she was, she always had been, a point for the police to tidy up in Charles's death.

"Neater," Lieutenant Welk had said, with the barest hesitation before the word; obviously it had not been neat enough before. It was equally obvious, now, that they would have thought about Sarah, and asked themselves where she had been during this fatal crisis in her new husband's life. A walk was such a vague and, the lieutenant's tone implied, peculiar thing.

Had he learned in the course of his inquiry that Frank, the elevator operator whom all the tenants liked and shielded from the superintendent's shrewish wife, was given to slipping around the corner for a quick beer on quiet evenings, leaving the elevator on self-service control? Had he been measuring Sarah for physical strength? Had he noticed that the alcove curtains were new? Of course he had, he noticed everything.

Sarah put her hands to her closed eyes and rubbed hard, and when she opened them again it was with the feeling of something erased, not permanently, but at least for now.

By one o'clock she had finished the trade ad and sent for a messenger. She knew perfectly well that her own headline would not appear—Mr. Eigel's ideas had always been handed down to him on stone—and that the air-brush lettering would say that Daintease girdled the world. As Mr. Eigel was Daintease, it was his privilege.

When the messenger had quavered off, Sarah went out herself. Her surface goal was lunch, but underneath that was the necessity for getting out of a dangerously closing shell. She walked north on Fifth Avenue, pausing to glance into shop windows, absorbing fragments of faces and moods, knowing herself to be like a very dry house plant. At the corner of Fifth and Thirty-ninth, waiting for a light to change, she met Jess Bertram.

Jess was a group head at the agency, and looked it. She had a smart, huddled, harried walk, and at the moment she was crouched into what fashion magazines were wont to call a Small Fur. Her dark dandelion head was bare—you could get away with that in a Small Fur—and she wore bamboo earrings and gloves that looked like mustard silk. Her opulent black-and-white coloring had always reminded Sarah of a very feminine skunk.

They knew each other with the false intimacy of women who meet only in conferences and elevators. "Sweetie!" said Jess, narrowing her eyes fondly at Sarah and then peering across the street in search of someone. "*How* is the bride? You look absolutely . . ." Wisely, she let that dwindle off. "We miss you terribly. They dredged up some journalism-school character for Supersheen and she's so fearsomely earnest that she'll have us all back on our ulcer diets yet."

Having raked the opposite street corner, she was now gazing inquisitively at Sarah. This was what Sarah had dreaded, this was the jump that had to be taken at once. "Jess, I'm sorry I didn't get around to telling people sooner. Charles is—he died in December."

But the light had changed at last, and a revving of motors and a chorus of horns drowned out the last of that. "He's absolutely stunning," said Jess Bertram, giving Sarah a look of respect. "I saw you both not long ago at that new place in the Village, but you were so wrapped up in each other that I didn't—" The face she had been waiting for caught her eye and she shrieked a greeting across the street, said hastily to Sarah, "Take care, sweetie," and was gone.

Sarah walked numbly away. People like Jess Bertram never waited for explanations, which was perhaps just as well. "That wasn't my husband, that was his best friend." Or, "We were actually talking about Charles's insurance."

Nevertheless, even knowing what it had been—a flight from shock on her part, a quiet Good Samaritan role on Harry Brendan's—she felt peculiarly appalled.

She was back at the apartment at a little after two, and in the lobby she met the superintendent's wife. Mrs. Carminio said anxiously, "What did he say?" and after a few blank inquiries on both sides the question resolved itself.

Mrs. Carminio's expert eye had seen through Lieutenant Welk's civilian clothes, and she had thought him a "higher-up," someone to check on the sergeant who had come the day before in response to her own report that the basement storeroom had been broken into.

"Or they tried to break in," said Mrs. Carminio with a vengeful air. "That's Mr. Carminio's night to—his night off, but he had a little touch of the flu and he came back early, and he heard them all right. He's got ears like a hawk. They was gone when he got there, but we can't have that, not in this building."

Sarah went on into the elevator, bemused at the suggestion that Mr. Carminio superintended other buildings in his spare time, and wouldn't mind their being burgled at all. It must, she thought, be a delicate decision to make. On the heels of that came the reminder that she must, some day, do something about Charles's things. She called them "things" to herself; she shrank away from the more exact itemizing. But what did people do? Give them to the superintendent? Call up a charitable organization?

In the apartment, by association, she went to the bedroom closet and took down Charles's briefcase and opened it.

It was stamped C.T. in small gold letters. His office had sent it home after, presumably, extracting what was necessary to the firm. There were a number of old letters to and from writers, and there was the handsome engagement book Sarah had given him.

She had to steel herself to open it, but she needn't have worried. Although she might have asked Charles to pick up bitters on his way home, or mail one of her letters, or do any other small personal thing, there was no trace of it here.

This contained appointments and notes about appointments, and that was all.

"Photo Herzogs. With cats? Williamson. Mrs. Armstead lunch, new biog. See Henrick."

There were a number of notes about Hollister, the best-selling inspirational writer on whose publicity Charles had worked so hard and so late during that last week. Or most of the time; on at least one occasion, the day he had told her he was going to Chicago to see Hollister, he had visited the psychiatrist instead. Sarah's mind presented her cruelly with the memory of how serene he had been after that, and how soundlessly he had slept—not because of exhaustion, as she had thought, but because he had shifted his burden, and told his tale of terror to someone whose business it was to take terrors apart and show their harmless component parts.

It was hard to get used to the fact of her name in Vollmer's full button mouth, the questions he must have asked Charles about her . . . No wonder Charles had given that hard explosive laugh when Sarah had asked him to see a psychiatrist, no wonder he had said, after his fourth cocktail, "Do you know, I think you're the last person I'd tell?"

This wouldn't do, it was only giving new life to the helpless bitterness she had thought was dead. Sarah turned a page as calmly as though she were being watched, and came upon "Lunch, H." Or was it a careless "K"?

Harry Brendan? Hunter Gideon? Kate Clemence? It was the first use of an initial she had come upon so far; all the other names had related to business and were meticulously written out—for his secretary's use, Sarah supposed. Her heart had begun to quicken, because this was the day of Charles's death.

She must be mistaken about its being one of them, because no one had said anything about having seen Charles only hours before he died. And it would be instinctive to say it, in exactly that way: "But I saw him only that day, at lunch . . ."

Someone in the office, then, whom Charles lunched with so frequently that an initial sufficed. Harold, Henry, Karl, or possibly a surname.

There were three other names below that, or rather two; one had been crossed out. Reeves, and then the indecipherable scoring of black pencil, and then Elliot.

Reeves. Elliot. Something twitched at Sarah's memory and then let go. For no good reason she thought of the woman murdered on the mink farm—but her name had been Braceway, and the man who had killed her was someone called Peck. Elliot was often a Christian name, but Reeves . . . betrayingly, her mind began to outfit them with other names and contexts, seen in the street or in newspaper ads. And who was the crossed-out man in between? Not that they mightn't as easily be women, but Charles had written Mrs. Armstead and, in another place, Miss J. Wing.

Why was she sitting so transfixedly still, wondering whether the police had seen this particular page in their routine investigation? They must have; they would have wanted to know about Charles's state of mind that day, and whether there had been any unusual development in that area of his life. And she already knew that they had checked with his office.

Nevertheless . . . it was not quite three-thirty. Sarah knew as she went to the phone exactly what she was doing: she was trying to get out from under. She wanted to prove, only to herself, that the thing Charles couldn't face, the thing that had snapped his reason, lay much deeper than the episode on the bluff, and she had been only an unconsciously-furnished scapegoat. An old tragedy, perhaps, in which people named Reeves and Elliot had been equally involved; a scar of some kind that his stepmother's death, and then the nurse's, had reawakened. . . .

She said to the switchboard voice that answered her, "Miss Ehrhardt, please."

Charles's secretary had been with him a number of years and she was, perhaps understandably in view of the circumstances, disposed to be cool to Sarah. She said that Mr. Trafton hadn't kept any lunch date that day because a conference had been called at shortly before twelve. He had asked her to bring his notes up to the conference room for him and when she left the office he had been dialling a number, presumably to cancel his lunch. He had gone out afterwards, well after one-thirty, but she really couldn't say. . . .

Sarah thanked her, and went transparently on. "There seem to be so many people to write, and a lot of details . . . have you an address for Mr. Reeves, or Mr. Elliot?"

". . . No," said Miss Ehrhardt's hesitating voice, with a frown in it. "I've been asked about that, but I really don't know. We published a Mr. Vernon Chase Elliot years ago, but he's with another house now and living in Santa Monica. In any case he was before Mr. Trafton's time, and there hasn't been any correspondence. I have no record at all of a Mr. Reeves."

But it was there in her voice, as it had been in Sarah's mind: the tiny bothered pause before certainty. Sarah said, "Well, thanks very much," and her disappointment must have been clear because Miss Ehrhardt, thawing rapidly, said, "I'm sorry I can't help, Mrs. Trafton. If there's anything else I can do . . ."

Sarah had not realized until she hung up how much she had been building on the identification of the two names in the appointment book. With a mind trained to the embroidering of fact, she had even evolved a situation that would have gnawed at Charles years after it happened: a fatal fall, the result of a joke or a dare, by a member of a party that had included Charles and Reeves and Elliot. Or any set of circumstances ending in a tragedy which he might have averted if he had not turned his back on it.

H, she thought, going back to the lunch date; H, or K. In the face of all her sensible arguments it was still Hunter or Harry or Kate Clemence. On closer inspection, she could see why Kate might have kept quiet about that. If she had been in New York again, and phoned Charles at his office instead of the apartment, it might have seemed a little awkward.

Hunter needn't have had any such scruples, nor Harry Brendan. But could Harry have spent that peculiarly indelible time with Sarah without mentioning the fact that he had seen Charles, or at any rate arranged to meet him, earlier that day? Yes, thought Sarah surprisedly, he could. He was a man who kept his own counsel; there was nothing sunny or open about him at all. It was, in fact, hard to conceive the authority to which Harry Brendan would feel obliged to explain anything.

Again, she had forgotten to thaw the lamb chops. Sarah looked hopelessly at them at five o'clock and, mindful of last night's frightful meal, went out to the delicatessen on Lexington with a small shopping list. On her way in she opened her mailbox. There was an anxious note from her sister in California, asking her to visit them, three advertisements which she dropped unopened into the wastebasket, and the letter from Bess Gideon which, if she had received it a day earlier or a day later, might have had quite a different effect.

vi

THE LETTER was typed, a detail which made Sarah instantly and unfairly suspicious. She typed most of her own letters—she had grown so used to thinking on a typewriter that the only things a pen would write readily for her were a check or a grocery list—but every other communication she had had from Bess Gideon had been in a round backhand.

As crisply and practically as though Sarah had never written to say that she did not want to sell the farm, Bess offered thirty thousand. True, Charles's father had paid only twenty-three when he bought it, but in view of all the improvements and the rising real-estate values on the South Shore, she thought thirty was fair. If Sarah would care to speak to her lawyer so that the necessary arrangements could be put in train . . .

That took care of the first paragraph. In the second, Charles's gold pocket watch had belonged to four generations of Traftons or Gideons. Of course, if Sarah had a particular attachment, they would all understand.

New paragraph. Perhaps Sarah remembered that Bess had

given Charles her small overnight case some time ago, to have the lock repaired at the shop where Charles had bought it. Bess didn't know when she might be in New York, but if Sarah would leave the case with the superintendent she could have someone pick it up without troubling Sarah.

The letter ended with the somehow preposterous suggestion that whenever Sarah happened to be up that way—on one of my periodic trips to Boston to buy a hat, perhaps? wondered Sarah—they would all be so glad to see her.

It was like a letter to a caretaker, polite but brisk, full of commissions and reminders. Or at least Sarah's tight nerves saw it that way.

Her first reaction was to stalk into the bedroom and get the gold watch from the bureau drawer where Charles had kept it, as though Bess Gideon were actually waiting there with her palm outstretched. And here was the overnight case, alligator and very handsome. What tremendous nuisances people could suggest in that offhand way. If Sarah left it with the superintendent and something happened to it—a scratch from one of their Siamese cats, for instance—or if the would-be burglar succeeded on his second try, Bess would hold her responsible until doomsday.

Her next impulse was to go straight to the telephone—but not now, while she was still in this militant frame of mind. Wait, think it over, remember that Bess, all of them for that matter were in a rather awkward position, living in a house that now belonged to a semi-stranger; naturally they would want to have something settled. And Charles had been variously nephew and cousin: remember that, too. She had known him for less than a year, and been his wife for only six weeks, whereas he had been, even if intermittently, a part of their lives.

They hadn't had time to think, at the funeral; they had been busy about telegrams and flowers and all the other merciful preoccupations that obscure, a little, what has actually happened. But they had had time by now. It would be only human for them to have said to each other, "It's certainly very odd. Married six weeks and then— You can't tell me it wasn't something to do with her."

Or had they known, had even one of them known, that in marrying Charles she was picking up a loaded gun?

And where had that idea come from, and why was she walking around the room so rapidly and distractedly? Because they wanted to give her a check and cut her completely away? That was reasonable enough, she had no great or abiding affection for them either.

But to be set adrift with the monstrous hypothesis of Charles driven to kill himself before she could kill him was something else again. She might have to live with that, but not if she could help it. Certainly not without trying to track down the two names nobody seemed to know anything about.

Reeves, Elliot. If it were the kind of involvement she imagined, Bess wouldn't tell her and neither would Kate Clemence. She wasn't sure about Hunter; he was an unknown quantity. But Milo's malice, and Evelyn's wagging tongue . . . She had trained herself not to think about Harry Brendan, and she didn't now.

After her dinner, much more calmly, she read the letter again. Then she went to the telephone and called Bess Gideon in Preston.

"Sarah!" It took Bess a moment to collect her wits and any kind of warmth. "How nice to hear from you. We've all been wondering about you, and I've thought of calling several times, but it seemed so sort of checking-up."

Sarah tucked that away for future inspection and said it had been thoughtful of Bess to write. She hadn't really had time to think about the farm, what with one thing and another, but now that she had a chance to get out of New York for a few days, would they have room for her if she came up?

Bess sounded instantly pleased and cordial, which meant nothing at all; she came of a generation which would administer ground glass if necessary but could never be merely rude. "When had you thought of coming? The sooner the better. Let's see, this is Tuesday . . ."

They settled on Thursday. Sarah said she could take the Clipper and then a cab from Route 128, but Bess said nonsense, Hunter would meet her. Milo's crow cawed suddenly in the background, and brought the long-distance strangeness surprisingly close.

The telephone at the farm was in the dining room. The walls were painted a soft clear yellow above the white dado, the huge fireplace was gray stone, black-and-white toile hung at the windows. The furniture was a deliberate minimum: mahogany table and chairs, radio-phonograph in a cabinet, telephone table and chair in one corner. There were never flowers there, even in the summer, only lemon leaves or ashy sprays of eucalyptus in a silver pitcher. The effect was of standing in a cube of cool uncluttered light.

Bess, at the telephone, would be signalling at the others with her thin expressive face: at Milo in a doorway with his eyebrows owlishly up, or Evelyn, who would have stopped doing the dinner dishes to see what this latest development was. Hunter Gideon . . . Sarah's mind tried to grasp at him, and couldn't. As though a tube had blown somewhere, the whole picture vanished and there was only Bess's voice saying something about the alligator case.

"Yes, I'll bring that. And the watch," said Sarah precisely. "Oh, and perhaps we'll have a chance to talk about something else while I'm there."

"Oh?" The wire seemed to hum with increased tautness, but Sarah probably imagined that. "Something about . . . ?"

The crow unloosed a barrage of croaks and clucks, providing a welcome cover. "Thursday, then," said Sarah, and was about to add goodbyes when Bess said brightly, "You just missed Harry Brendan and Kate. They dropped in for a few minutes on their way somewhere. They'll be so pleased when they hear . . ."

Will they indeed, thought Sarah, staring blankly at the rug—but it was not, on second thought, the vacant remark it seemed. Bess wasn't given to vacant conversation. This was notice that the ranks were being closed.

She hadn't realized how difficult it would be to invite herself on these people. Her fingers still felt stiff from their grip on the receiver, the muscles around her mouth must have been producing a smile to go with her voice all that time.

Thursday . . .

Sarah went through Charles's appointment book again, without finding anything more to wonder about. The H or K of the unkept lunch date—or had it been kept, later?—remained an open question. She half expected Miss Ehrhardt to call and say that she had dug Reeves and Elliot out of the files and they were free-lance photographers, or locksmiths, or friendly newspaper contacts, but Miss Ehrhardt did not.

She wondered whether Lieutenant Welk was still puzzling over her walk on the night of Charles's death, but as he neither came nor called there was no way of knowing.

While she packed, she looked for and failed to find the framed snapshot of Charles, a fact which made her coolly and impersonally angry. Surely there was a point where helpfulness stopped and license set in.

She talked to the superintendent and assured him that she would arrange some disposition of her husband's suitcases when she returned. She did her nails and had her hair cut shiningly short, but it did not occur to her until shortly before train time that she had been preparing not so much for a visit as—translated from the female—a descent behind the enemy lines.

Hunter Gideon met her as arranged at Route 128.

The train got in half an hour late, which put Sarah at a disadvantage; added to that was a thin icy rain that froze as it fell and must have made the fifteen-mile trip from Preston that much more of a nuisance. She began to apologize while Hunter was still crossing the tracks toward her, tall and spare in oilskins, the sheen of the rain seeming to sharpen his brusque high-cheekboned face.

"No trouble at all," he said, collecting her bags. "How've you been? You look like the very devil." He paused to peer at the ranked cars. "Now, damn it, where are we?"

After that little spate of talk, which Hunter himself seemed surprised and chagrined at, they retired into a mutual silence. Sarah was caught in the half-hypnotized fatigue with which long train trips always afflicted her, and Hunter had to concentrate on the icy road and freezing windshield.

Ask him right now if he had had an appointment with Charles that day? No, thought Sarah, and justified her instinctive refusal, here in the confinement of the car, by the darkness which would conceal any reaction. But he had seen the half-turn of her head toward him and turned his own inquiringly.

"How—are the pheasants?" Too late, she realized that the question might sound proprietary, but Hunter seemed relieved at the introduction of a topic that would keep them going for a while. They had had one casualty, he said; a black-throated Golden cock, one of his mother's favorites, had been killed by a mink. There had also been an incident of another kind: the Silver cock had scratched and bitten a neighborhood child who had teased and then loosed him.

Even with the sudden oppression of the mink farm upon her again, Sarah was amazed. "You mean a pheasant will actually attack a child?"

"Not most breeds. Silvers are belligerent by nature—they've been known to pursue people who've teased or harmed them into houses when they're really aroused. They're big birds, and they've got a tremendous wing span and spurs like knives. And unfortunately Long John, the one that went after the boy, had lost his bit and could use his beak into the bargain."

Sarah remembered the bits some of the pheasants had worn, tiny metal rings inserted through the beaks to prevent pecking and defeathering, particularly when a pair were crated for shipping. Charles had explained that to her on one of those limpidly gold afternoons. The memory struck her into a silence that lasted most of the way home, except for an occasional, "Slippery there," and, "Yes, wasn't it?" If

Sarah had known the man beside her either less or better, she might have asked a number of questions. As it was, convention, and the peculiar relationship in which they stood to each other, assumed that they were a good deal more at ease than they were.

They had reached the house, long and yellow-lit in the dark, its ice-coated rail fence glittering briefly in the headlights as Hunter turned in at the gate. He drove into the barn, braked expertly just before the stacked fire-wood, and said without turning his head, "Have you found out yet why Charles killed himself?"

It was not so much the question itself as the tone of it —the tenseness, the sudden ripping away of politeness—that brought Sarah's gaze shockedly around. In the carving of light from the dashboard he didn't look unlike a rather bold pheasant himself; there was the profile spare to sharpness, the poised and total stillness, testing the very air.

Not a man to share secrets with. "Well, unsound mind . . ." said Sarah, deliberately bewildered, and wondered, when he switched off the lights, whether the darkness hid a look of contempt.

Bess Gideon kissed her cheek lightly, Evelyn was effusive, Milo said whimsically, "Meanwhile, back on the pharm . . ." Somehow he managed to make the spelling clear and to invest it, like most of his utterances, with a secret amusement. Sarah shook his warm plump hand and barely avoided wiping her own on her coat.

Hunter made drinks during the little flurry of arrival. Bess said with apology that they were having the guest room re-papered and it was a mess; would Sarah mind using Charles's old room instead, just for this visit?

Sarah said, “Not at all. Anywhere,” and wondered whether this was a test of sentiment or a challenge or nothing but what it seemed. Bess was smiling at her so measuringly.

The older woman had undergone what Sarah knew was her daily metamorphosis. A man came once a week to clean the pheasant pens and chicken house and make any needed repairs, but apart from that Bess took care of the birds herself. She dressed in slacks that suited her lean figure but usually had a tear or a patch or a streak of paint somewhere, and someone’s discarded plaid shirt with the sleeves rolled up. With work gloves on, a pail in each hand and her short gray hair blown about or rained upon, she had always looked to Sarah like a character actress working hard on a role.

At six o’clock she seemed to change her skin as well as her clothes. She was invariably in slender unadorned black —with no distraction, the eye went to and stayed upon her haggard and faintly satirical face—and Evelyn, who had looked overdressed all day, now looked underdressed.

By tacit agreement, nothing of what they were so separately bent upon was mentioned. Hunter made drinks again, and the freezing rain changed to sleet and bounced microscopically off the windows—how black windows were in the country. Milo, with a poker-faced pedantry, told a story that Sarah was amazed Bess would tolerate; she reminded herself, not even pretending to smile, that he was a man with whom insult passed for wit and vulgarity for humor.

What had she thought she could find out here? Evelyn had sat down beside her and was confiding the domestic problems of a friend who had recently moved to Jefferson City—small wonder, thought Sarah unkindly—but they corresponded and the friend had been so upset to hear about Charles.

Charles. Surprisingly unreal himself now, but leaving behind a very real burden. How could he have . . . ? Anger and hurt, or perhaps the cocktails after the train trip and the drive here, caught up on Sarah without warning. She said into the smooth flow of Evelyn's voice, "Yes, that must be awfully hard for them. Is it—" she could not help putting her palms against her cheeks "—very hot in here? I feel . . ."

Evelyn's gaze expanded alertly; she was, thought Sarah a little wildly, the only person she had ever seen who could flex her eyeballs. And an idea was dawning on Evelyn, visibly. "Are you— You don't think you could be—?"

Sarah stared at her in perplexity until the whisper and the woman-to-woman air sank in. "Pregnant?" she said. "Oh dear, no. That would be awkward, wouldn't it?"

It fell resoundingly into an attentive silence. Hunter turned his head hastily away, apparently to ward off a sneeze. Milo slid his glasses to the end of his nose and peered roundly at Sarah over them. Bess said with aplomb, "It is hot in here—look at the thermostat, will you, Hunter? And Evelyn, I think the roast must be done."

The roast was not only done but thoroughly grayed. Evelyn, who took care of the meals as Bess took care of the pheasants, was an elaborately bad cook of the fruit-salad school. Nothing was allowed to stand by itself. Peas had to have milk added to them, potatoes were tortured out of and back into their shells with a garnishing of something peculiar. Any oven-cooked meat was either plastered with or surrounded by some foreign element, usually fruit.

Sarah moved her fork delicately and questingly, and came

upon what might have been an apricot. She sat beside Milo, who handed her peas with a murmured, "Let's see, you're eating for one, aren't you?" She bore that in silence, because she had brought it on herself in that unstrung moment, but when Bess moved shakers about and said, "These are all pepper, I think," Sarah pushed her chair back and said rapidly, "Let me."

She had been at the house often enough to know where the table things were kept, and even an instant alone was surcease. In the kitchen she took down a shaker, sprinkled salt experimentally into her palm, turned to go back and saw the man at the window.

He must have been standing quite close to the glass, in fact pressing against the pane, because otherwise his normal expression would have been distorted beyond belief. Sarah glanced fleetingly at dark hair dipping over a low forehead, splayed nose, mouth stretched in the kind of grin children usually accomplished by the use of two fingers, and was out of the kitchen before the tap could sound at the door.

Bess frowned, Hunter said, "I'll go," and did. The door in the kitchen opened and a low interchange began. Evelyn turned her head listeningly and then devoted herself to her dinner; the man in the kitchen was obviously someone of no interest. Bess said, "Tell me, Sarah, have you seen that new Italian movie there's such a furor about?" and presently Hunter came back and resumed his dinner without a word.

Someone wanting to buy a pheasant, explained Sarah to herself, or wanting to trade, as pheasant fanciers always seemed to be doing. Or perhaps someone paying for quail eggs; she thought she had heard the clink of coins. He had only frightened her because she was nervous anyway and, a city dweller, not used to faces framed against the dark.

They had coffee in the living room, and when Evelyn rose to take out the cups Sarah went with her. She said lightly to Bess's protest that she had been sitting too long on the train, but it wasn't that, nor even the faint compassion for anyone whose nightly ritual, taken for granted, was the doing of all the dishes and pots and pans.

Evelyn washed and Sarah dried, at the other woman's insistence. Over a rush of water, Sarah said casually, "Who was the man who came during dinner?"

Evelyn's allergic rubber-gloved hands deposited a vegetable dish in the rack. "He helps Bess with the pheasants, and I suppose he forgot his pay. Or else Bess didn't have the cash when he left last time. She'd just paid for a pair of blue-eared Manchurians."

Something about the cool air of censure not quite withheld surprised Sarah. She dried the vegetable dish and put it away, thinking back to the sunburned college boy she had seen the last time she was here. "He's new, isn't he?"

"Well, new here," said Evelyn. "Isn't it awful the way some cups get dark at the bottom? When you think of the prices they charge. Actually, he's been around here a long time, in fact—" she turned from the sink, stripping off her gloves "—he used to work at the mink farm down the road. Peck, his name is."

Something in Sarah's mind jumped unpleasantly. "*Peck . . . ?*"

"I see you know about him," said Evelyn. She sounded almost pleased. "He's the man they arrested for that murder on the mink farm. You know, the nurse. Miss Braceway.

vii

SARAH HADN'T needed reminding. Two echoes came back: of Kate Clemence saying over tea in New York, "They've caught the man who killed the nurse. He used to work on the mink farm . . ." and Charles, later, "My God. Poor Peck. . . ."

And he had slept soundly that night and the next.

Evelyn was still watching her with that curiously pleasurable air. "The police held him for a while, but then it turned out that he'd been somewhere else when it was done and they had to let him go. Charles used to try and find jobs for him and I suppose Bess felt sorry for him when he came around looking for work."

Why was Evelyn liking this? Was it a taste for tragedy, or merely the unfamiliar sensation of being listened to with sharp interest? Sarah said slowly, "If it wasn't Peck—" and Evelyn blew into her rubber gloves. The limp red fingers became frighteningly lively, a meddlesome pair of hands capable of anything, and died again. "I don't suppose they'll ever find out now," said Evelyn in an abstracted way. "They were so sure it was Peck that they weren't looking for anyone else, and he's had plenty of time to disappear."

The mink farm, Sarah was thinking with sudden attention. Although it wasn't visible from here and there was apparently no interchange between the two houses, it was a thread that appeared with surprising constancy in the pattern of these people's lives. Miss Braceway had died there. One of the minks had killed a black-throated Golden cock. And here tonight was Peck, ex-employee . . .

She said with a lift of excitement, "Who owns the mink farm?"

"People named Hopkins," said Evelyn, quashing this possibility, but Sarah had met her gaze first and the letdown —Hopkins, not Reeves or Elliot—was lost in shock.

What a vast mistake it had been to be sorry for Evelyn, or even to dismiss her as a long-playing bore. Somewhere, thought Sarah, seeing the shrewd cold eyes for the first time, Evelyn was keeping a list of just such people, and it seemed entirely possible for a second that she would pay them all back.

But then Evelyn said in one of her random rushes, "This friend I was telling you about has the most awful trouble with her hands, too. She tried everything, and do you know what the doctor finally told her? He said . . ." and Sarah thought that she must have been mistaken after all.

She went early to bed, up the twisting back stair that led out of the dining room.

Bess had known where to stop, aesthetically and financially, when it came to this region of the house, a long narrow steeply peaked room that overran the dining room and kitchen. It had been whitewashed, and the one end window curtained in blue, but there was no attempt to hide the chimney that thrust up in the middle of it, nor the cobwebbed chests and trunks piled at the far end near the arching door that opened onto the barn loft.

The habitable end, on the near side of the chimney, held a bed, night table and lamp, braided rug, and a pine bureau, beautifully waxed under a shadowy mirror. Sarah's bags stood at the foot of the bed, along with the portable heater Hunter had plugged in when he brought them up.

Sarah turned the heater off, got into nightgown and robe, and went cautiously through the connecting door into the guest room. As Bess had said, the furniture was piled and wallpaper lay about in great curls on the floor. The bath that went with it was intact and she brushed her teeth, washed her pale unfamiliar face and went to bed.

Charles's bed. But then, as she knew, a great deal of juggling went on at the farm in the way of sleeping quarters—the living room couch opened up, so did the one in the study beyond—and it was possible that Miss Braceway had slept here during her tenure. Must have, because what was now the guest room had once been occupied by Charles's stepmother.

And what had her maiden name been?

Sarah's mind started in its grim circle again, but the blankets were warm, the sheets had a dried-in-the-wind fragrance. The sleet had stopped, and so had the house sounds below her. Imperceptibly, she went to sleep.

In what seemed a wink she was awake again, heart hammering; for one ghastly instant she expected to hear Charles cry out in the clenching grip of nightmare. But what her groping senses strained out of the darkness was quite different: a curious ripping sound, a soft plop, the creak of a board. All in the room with her, quite near, and all, she realized, long moments ago; it had taken awareness that interval to break through the barrier of sleep.

"Yes?" she said with the boldness of fright, and then, "Who is it?" and sat up with a deliberate thrashing of sheets before she reached for the light switch. It took courage to press it because who knew, in this room where Charles had slept, what sly shadow might be cast upon the wall by someone just out of sight, someone just around the corner of understanding?

But there was no other presence, and no shadow except her own when she made herself get out of bed and look behind the chimney. Nor was there any sound other than the contact of her bare feet with the floor planks. The very stillness had a difficult quality, as though whoever had been here was now standing somewhere else, breath held, listening as she listened.

Sarah broke out of her own rigidity. Nothing could have made her walk the length of the room to the loft door, swallowed in darkness; it was probably unlocked but she was going to get out of here right away. She put on robe and slippers and turned to see what it was that had waked her.

The plop had been her handbag, on the bureau when she switched off her lamp, now on the floor. A mouse might conceivably have done that, but a mouse could not have opened Bess's alligator travelling case and investigated the watermelon silk lining with such violence that the shirring was torn in one place. Sarah stood staring blankly down at it, and it was a measure of her own shock that she only wondered how she was going to explain the damage to Bess.

Tiptoeing, she went down the small stair, through the black dining room and into the living room, the core of this sprawling house. The lamp she found by touch rocked noisily on its base but it went on, summoning up a chair and a dwindling funnel of red oriental rug, the arched shadows of the pheasant feathers above the doorway, the mantel clock that said ten after two. The black windows, surprised into color again, twinkled serenely back at her.

Sarah left the lamp on and stretched herself out on the couch, trying vainly to find a comfortable place for her head. With physical fright gone, and the primitive reaction to having been approached unaware, she began to wonder why whoever had wanted something from her handbag or luggage had waited until that inconvenient hour. After all, there had been all evening—

But there hadn't. Hunter had started to take her bags upstairs shortly after she was in the house, but Bess had asked him to make cocktails and the bags had stood at the foot of the stairs until just before she went up to bed. After cocktails and dinner she had been in the kitchen with Evelyn, and from the sink you could look directly past the jog that contained Milo's crow and across the dining room to the stairway door. It would have been an awkward place to get at.

And what had she said to Bess, after the first greetings were over? "I remembered your case, and the watch . . ." But Hunter had carried the case upstairs with her things—not knowing it was his mother's? Or politely waiting for Sarah to turn it over?

Whoever it was had wanted something of Charles's, and had thought it might be in the case. Sarah was as sure of that as she was of her own rapidly stiffening neck. Whatever else these people might be they weren't thieves, after her wallet or whatever jewelry she might own. Unless . . . Peck?

But a man who had just been released after being held

on suspicion of murder would hardly risk recapture for theft, particularly on such a dubious quest. It was too bad, because Peck's villainous face made him such a believable scapegoat.

Sarah removed herself to a chair, tucked her robe around her cold ankles, and composed herself to remember what odds and ends of Charles's she might have included in her packing. Because something of his was bothering somebody here, and it wasn't anything that could be asked for openly, like the handed-down watch. . . .

The crowing of the Silkie rooster, a gunshot to city ears, woke her when the living room was turning an icy blue. She switched off the now-diminished lamp and went, stiff with cold and discomfort and sleepiness, back up to the attic room and to bed.

Milo had killed a mink during the night.

It was a matter of great triumph to everybody, and Sarah viewed the stiff caramel corpse with the rest. She had no compassion for the mink, which was only an expensive rodent and would have died by cyanide gas anyway, but she flinched from the exhibition of the short heavy stick Milo had used. There was blood on the end; she supposed that a closer examination, which Bess seemed quite willing to make, would reveal a few short hairs.

From his pride and his countless retelling of the details, Milo might have slain a sabre-toothed tiger, Sarah thought. He had been waked in the night by toothache—here he exhibited a molar to anyone who cared to look—and he had gone downstairs for some brandy to rinse it with. He didn't know what had made him think about the prowling mink of a few nights before, but as he was wakeful anyway he had thrown on a coat and gone out into the barn, picking up on his way the flashlight that was kept in the passage. He had no thought of going outside, not with his toothache in the bitter cold, but three of the pheasant pens opened off the stable.

And there was the mink. Sarah had not thought of Milo as a gifted teller of tales, but when he waggled his soft plump hands the mink came alive, supple, almost rippling, trying to slip through the wire mesh that protected the pheasants. It had been so intent in its greed, or perhaps so mesmerized by the flashlight beam, that not even the noise of Milo's approach had diverted it from the appetizing cock—pale gold satin with a black-masked white face—that roosted docilely only a few feet away.

"Whango," said Milo, hefting the stick, and that was when Sarah turned her head away, saying, "What time was this?"

They all looked at her as attentively as though the mink had spoken. "Twoish," said Milo, sliding his glasses down his nose and looking at her over them. "Were you awake in your bower, Sarah? I wish I'd known; you could have held the flashlight for me."

But Sarah had had time to think, and to realize that any mention of what had happened in the night would make her position here completely untenable—and was that, just possibly, the point? She said indifferently, "Not really awake, but I had a notion I'd heard something."

Which one of them had moved secretly about her room and knew she was lying? Bess had turned away and was feeding lettuce to a sweet-faced brownish hen which, unlike the violently snatching Silvers and the dartingly shy Japanese Coppers, took the morsels gently from her fingers. Evelyn was looking at the dead mink thoughtfully, as though measuring it for a scarf; Milo, seeing that the general interest had flagged a little, gazed around at them all and stood his stick in a corner of the stable. Hunter, hatted and coated for his morning departure for Boston and looking almost military among the rest of them, took a step toward the car, nodded back at the mink, and said in a clipped voice, "You don't suppose Peck's letting them out, to get back at Hopkins?"

There was a shocked silence as he left, and a few little curls of gray on the icy air as mouths opened involuntarily. Then Bess said violently, "Peck would never—besides, he's a country man and he'd know exactly where the mink would—"

The second argument was no more convincing than the first; in fact, it was disastrously less so. It outlined an almost classic scheme of revenge, Sarah thought: letting one person's mink loose to kill another's pheasants. Everybody lost, because the bludgeoned mink pelt would hardly be salable and even if it had not savaged the pheasant Bess Gideon would have eaten a neighbor sooner than one of her own beautiful birds.

Peck might harbor a grudge against Hopkins because he had been fired from the mink farm; Sarah turned her mind wilfully away from the one thing he might want to pay the Gideons back for. She was relieved when Kate Clemence arrived to borrow some sugar.

Kate had looked smart but ill at ease in New York; here in her own setting she had regained her magnificent, cope-with-anything calm. She was tall, and she ought to have looked masculine and muscular in the man's beige weatherproof parka, its hood up to show only an uneven fringe of black hair, but she didn't. It was a tribute to her that they were all diverted from the unpleasant notion that still hung on the air.

She greeted Sarah with a politeness that might have passed for warmth if nobody was listening. She said to Bess when she asked for the sugar, "I could do very nicely without it, but"—she grimaced out of what seemed to be habit—"you know Rob." Rob was evidently the brother Charles had mentioned, and well known to the Gideons, although Sarah had never seen him. "What are you all standing around and freezing for?"

The mink was exhibited, and Milo's tale retold. Kate said with unflattering surprise, "Well, good for you, Milo!" and Milo answered modestly, "Oh, come, I'm not all brain."

"You'll have coffee, won't you, Kate? Even Rob can wait five minutes. But first come and see my Manchurians, although they won't have settled down yet; I only got them yesterday . . . You haven't seen them either, Sarah," said Bess, and in spite of the afterthought quality of the invitation Sarah went with them.

The stable had been shadowed, and the silver-polished morning broke upon her like a wave of sound. After the night of freezing rain and sleet, light lay along every twig of every tree, gates and pens were glittering, the grass shattered crisply underfoot. The pheasants, unperturbed by the cold, made patterns of warmth and motion as they began to pace at the sight of Bess.

The blue-eared Manchurians were in the end pen of the row against the pines. Sarah thought at once that every other hen on the place must be hating this one, because instead of the usual quiet variations of brown she wore her mate's soft slate blue, arced with white at the sides of the head.

Only his spurs set the cock apart. They were dowager-like birds, moving with calm slow dignity.

"Aren't they lovely?" said Bess pleasedly. The water in the rimmed holder had frozen lightly although she had put it out less than an hour ago. She opened the door of the pen and broke the film of ice with a gloved finger. The Manchurians retreated a little, but without haste. "I'm not sure about this end spot for them," Bess said, frowning as she closed the door. "The man I bought them from had them more enclosed."

Kate considered. "You could put up pliofilm. Or you could move the Reeves."

Bess laughed dryly. "*You* could move the Reeves, thank you. Frightful-tempered things. I only got them because I wanted something that came into color the first year."

Unnoticed, Sarah went back into the house. Evelyn had made fresh coffee and was setting out cups and saucers; she said over her shoulder, "Kate's coming in, isn't she?"

"Yes, in a minute. They're looking at the Manchurians." How peculiar her voice sounded, but then it had to filter through the wild amusement that filled her head. "Evelyn, has Bess any Elliots?"

"Now there's the sugar Kate wants . . . Elliots? Yes, those kind of dark gold ones in the stable. You didn't get chilled out there, did you, Sarah?"

Reeves and Elliot. Not menacing figures in some hidden segment of Charles's life, when he wrote down their names on that last day, but pheasants on a farm two hundred and fifty miles away.

viii

It was mid-morning before Sarah got an opportunity to give Bess the travelling case and gold watch.

She had sewn the tear in the shirred lining of the case, managing with a great deal of difficulty to get the dangling pink thread through a needle, and although the repair job was far from expert it wasn't noticeable at a casual glance. Then, because it occurred to her that someone might have thought she would put the gold watch in the suitcase, to be handed over in one gesture to Bess, she took the watch from a compartment in her handbag and opened the back. It shone emptily at her, and although there was another inner casing, that was empty too. She supposed that she ought to have felt ridiculous even in looking, but she did not.

Bess said, "Thanks so much, Sarah; the travelling case was a birthday present from Charles last year. You're absolutely sure you don't mind about the watch? It's one of those foolish family things but I suppose we ought to keep up tradition and hand it on to Hunter."

Who looks, said Sarah silently, like not having anybody to hand it on to after him. Why? He would be attractive to women, with those cool eyes in the weathered face, and further enhanced by his very inaccessibility, like a fruit at the top of a thorny tree.

They were upstairs in Bess's room, at her suggestion; she was clearly creating the opportunity for a talk to settle the future ownership of the farm. Not surprisingly, it was a brisk and almost austere room, requiring a minimum of care. The books in a neat student-like pile on the bedside table seemed to be mostly about game birds in captivity. The only wall decoration was a Currier and Ives print of a quail with her progeny, entitled "The Cares of a Family."

"This is all quite difficult, isn't it?" said Bess with an air of candor. "Talking business like this—but then it does have to be talked about. What do you think about the price for the place?"

Two could play at candor, and Sarah, at the agency, had learned to smile when she was bubbling with rage, look enthralled while smothered yawns were forcing tears to her eyes, use, straight-facedly, the terms to which advertising conversation had been reduced. She said, "I'm being foolish, I know, but it's just that Charles loved this place so . . . I'm all for things going on just as they have been, but if you won't have that, couldn't we arrive at a rent?"

"Charles did love the farm, yes. As—if I can say this without being offensive—a visitor. It was always very comfortable for him when he came here, and I don't imagine it occurred to him how many wheels went around to make it that way. Under normal circumstances he would have outlived me, and so the question never came up, but I'm quite sure he would have wanted me to have the farm."

Was it the total arrogance it seemed? Perhaps not. Sarah said with a rueful air, "When I make *my* will I'm going to have everything perfectly clear in it, to cover all eventualities."

Bess was far too self-controlled to react to that. "I only broach it at all because, of course, you would never want to live here."

"Probably not. Somehow or other I haven't been able to make plans yet."

"You'll marry again," said Bess in a tone of certainty. "Perhaps that sounds shocking now but you're only—twenty-four, twenty-five? Of course you will. But after all you only got here last night, so let's shelve all this until you've had a little more time to get your bearings. Oh, and wasn't there something else you wanted to talk to me about?"

Sarah had had time to think about this answer. She looked at her hands for a long moment of silence before she said, "Charles was going to a psychiatrist before he died." (Odd that Hunter was the only one who had ever said bluntly, "killed himself." The rest of them skirted the issue, as though Charles had had a respectable disease and the very best of attention at the end.)

"A psychiatrist?" Bess sounded and looked aghast. "What for—what happened?"

"I only found out a few days ago myself," said Sarah steadily. "I was hoping you might be able to tell me."

Bess got abruptly off the bed where she had been sitting and walked to the window, presenting her back to Sarah. "I can't imagine Charles . . . didn't he give you any clue? Didn't the psychiatrist?"

"None."

"But it doesn't seem possible. Not with Charles. Of course, he grew up without a mother, and his father's death

—heart, as you probably know, although none of us had suspected it—was a considerable shock. But even so . . ."

"He was quite fond of his stepmother, wasn't he?"

"Nina. Oh, very. We all were. Still . . . Sarah, this is terribly upsetting. To think that Charles might have had some frightful problem his family didn't know about . . ."

Touché, thought Sarah wryly, and rose on cue. "I'll be down in a few minutes," said Bess gravely; the implication was that while Sarah might be cool about it she herself needed time to absorb this fresh shock. As well she may, thought Sarah, trying to be fair, but just then Bess opened the door so abruptly that the draught acted on the door opposite, releasing the catch and showing a slice of the bedroom inside.

Sarah knew instinctively that it was Milo and Evelyn's; Hunter could never have lived in the clutter she only remembered later. At the moment, all she saw was an easel, holding a very bad portrait of a seated woman preparing to wash her hair. There was a basin, and something in the background, but what caught the eye hypnotically was the loosed and tumbled-down hair, a crude beautiful red-yellow. The perspective was bad, the body lines stiff; the hair seemed glowingly alive.

Bess drew an audible breath, which might have been surprise—the portrait looked new and unfinished—or anger, or chagrin at her own suddenness. She said evenly enough, "Milo isn't much of an artist, but that's supposed to be Nina. She did have lovely hair. Watch the stair carpet, Sarah, it slides in spots, and I live in fear that somebody will trip."

Mechanically, Sarah had given Charles's stepmother a comforting bosom, a lot of sensible understanding, perhaps even a whiff of lavendar sachet. According to Milo's portrait —she would not have been more surprised to come upon Milo himself in a sarong—Nina Trafton could not have been much older than Charles, her bosom had not been designed for stepsons, and she was probably more attuned to Lanvin than to lavendar.

Evelyn had been gotten to; she avoided Sarah's eye when Sarah found her in the kitchen. "Do you like tuna fish?"

"Yes," said Sarah unwisely and then, with craft, "I've just been talking to Bess. It must have been awfully sad about Mrs. Trafton—Charles's stepmother, I mean."

"Yes, it was quite . . . I have noodles," said Evelyn nervously to herself, "and I have pineapple."

"Was she sick long?" asked Sarah, ignoring the frightful implication of what Evelyn was saying, and Evelyn looked at her almost with relief. "No, but she wasn't very strong, and the doctor warned us right away when pneumonia set in. There was a history of lung weakness, and I think he was surprised when she even—hand me that bowl, would you?"

Sarah did. She repeated invitingly, "When she even what?" but Evelyn had lost her last night's eagerness to talk. "Rallied," she said shortly.

It was obviously a fill-in word, but then this was a conversation Evelyn could hardly be expected to enjoy, not when her husband was painting the subject of it. And yet she seemed more—muzzled than resentful. Sarah watched her drop noodles into boiling water and butter a large casserole. "Was Charles here at the time?"

"Oh, yes. He was in the Boston office then and he used to come out for weekends. Toward the end he came on the train every night. He worshipped Nina, and I think he knew that she wasn't going to get better."

Worship was an odd word between contemporaries; surely the woman in the portrait couldn't have been more than five or six years older than Charles. Not with that long vivid hair . . . Sarah stood in silence for so long that the noodles began to froth over. People still died of pneumonia, in spite of all the new drugs, and pulmonary weakness often hid behind that glowing look of health. Besides, Sarah thought, faintly horrified at the direction her mind was taking, there couldn't have been any hocus-pocus, not in such a small town. The fact that the woman who had nursed Nina Trafton was also dead, but by violence, was just an unfortunate juxtaposition of events.

She realized that in between watching the noodles and draining the tuna fish Evelyn was giving her a number of furtive, tempted glances, much as a woman on a strict diet might keep eyeing a box of chocolates. Evelyn had something interesting to say, but had been told not to say it. Could her reluctant self-control be weakened?

Sarah said, "Had she and Charles's father been married long when he died?" and drew a complete blank. Evelyn said without interest, "About three years."

"This is rather a damp climate, isn't it, for someone with chest problems? But I suppose Nina was used to it if she grew up here."

Evelyn's sandy lashes dropped. She was not reaching out for the chocolates; the chocolates were coming to her. "Actually she was from somewhere in the West. Charles's father met her when she was visiting relatives here . . . she was Nina Clemence then."

Behind Sarah, so suddenly that he must have been standing there for some time, Milo said, "Learning to cook, Sarah? Or may we hope that you're teaching Evelyn?"

Did he never say anything without a sting in it? Evelyn smiled obediently, and Sarah moved a deliberate step away from the face that seemed too intimately close. "Just gossiping," she said sweetly. "As women do."

Milo gave her a sharp sparkling look. "I trust you brought some fresh gossip with you? It's hard to get in the country."

"You can't have been reading many best-sellers lately," said Sarah. "The city isn't in it with the country. Can I help, Evelyn, or would you rather I got out of your way?"

Why had Charles never told her that the stepmother he had been so fond of had been a relative of Kate's?

There was no sign of Bess. Sarah got her coat, put cigarettes in her pocket, and went outside. The day was still locked in a gray-and-crystal cold. She visited the beautiful, bad-tempered Reeves, trailing their magnificent tails, and the ruddy, white-breasted Elliots who seemed scarcely more amenable. Like all the pens, theirs were equipped with litter, a metal trough filled with turkey pellets, a water-holder.

What name in his appointment book had been scratched out between Reeves and Elliot? Japanese Copper, Silver, Lady Amherst? It could only have been scratched out because it did not measure up to some requirement, or answer some possibility in Charles's mind, on the day his reason broke.

It couldn't have anything to do with selling or breeding these pheasants, because he had never had a hand or even an interest in that; it was Bess's domain. Bess had spoken of wheels going around, and it was much more evident in the winter than in the summer. Sarah knew that the property was a working farm, for tax purposes, and that it was Milo's job to see that whatever requirements that meant were met.

The annual pheasant hatch alone was surprisingly profitable, the combined chicks averaging about eighty. The hay in the huge back fields was cut and sold every year, and regular shipments of tiny speckled eggs from the Japanese king quail went out to devotees in Newport, Miami, Bar Harbor. Bess kept a constant supply in the refrigerator for their own consumption, pickled in beet juice and vinegar, and served them on toothpicks with cocktails. They weren't much bigger than robin's eggs, but as much more delicate than a hen's egg as a hen's is than a duck's.

. . . She had reached the hickory tree where she and Charles had paused for a cigarette that day in their flight from Evelyn's friend. Her ears were cold; she dug automatically into her pocket but there wasn't a scarf, only cigarettes. The scarf, that other time, and the bluff . . . eerily, as though memory had summoned it up, a stir of wind sent the iced hickory branches crashing lightly together over Sarah's head.

She could see the bluff now, through the winter-stripped barrier of birch and aspen and hickory. Before it had been hidden in the leafage of summer. Anyone could have observed them without being seen himself, could have watched that bizarre trick of the wind with the silk square, could have said to Charles later, "Maybe it was her idea of a joke, but she threw it all right. . . ."

Her mind had gone in a useless circle last night, but it stopped now on a point of clarity. Charles's nightmare had been born here before she ever met him. Why else would he have written down, completely out of context and in a strictly-business appointment book, the names of three pheasants, one eliminated? And it had something to do with his stepmother—why else would he, otherwise so open and uncomplicated, have shut even her maiden name into a private compartment?

Carefully now; examine this. Remember Charles's strained face on her very first visit here, when Kate Clemence had told him that the dead woman on the mink farm was the nurse, Miss Braceway. Skip to New York, after their marriage, and his deep dreamless relief that her killer had been caught.

He had not been personally attached to Miss Braceway, so that could only mean the wiping out of some secret fear. That someone else had killed the nurse? That there was reason for someone to kill her?

The relaxedness and the absence of nightmare had lasted for two days before the torment resumed. And if one message from the farm had brought about that calm, it stood to reason that another message from the same source had destroyed it. And twice in that strange blurred week, she had thought she saw faces from Preston—Hunter's, once, and Harry Brendan's, and she had looked endlessly at Milo's round horn-rimmed glasses. It had seemed like a trick of her nerves then. It didn't now.

Suppose—although supposition was dangerous and wilfully constructed on air—suppose that someone had come to Charles (H? K?) and told him that the police had released Peck because he had an ironclad alibi for the time of the murder. That would leave the whole thing wide open again, an area of horror for Charles because the people who were closest to him could be concerned in it.

None of it explained what he had told the psychiatrist, except a theory that seemed to Sarah untenable: that he was in fact frightened of someone and knew he needed help if he were to preserve his marriage, but that at the last moment, in Vollmer's office, he had put up Sarah as a smoke screen against something worse.

What could be worse than a conviction that your wife was planning to push you from a height?

Sarah walked rapidly back to the house, face aching from the cold. It was hardly conceivable that a fear of such magnitude had been totally unsuspected by Charles's family and close friends. In that case their silence on the subject of his motive for suicide had not been tact but secrecy, and a willingness to let her bear the full responsibility.

Perhaps she had not understood the mortal danger in which Charles stood from himself, but the burden belonged right here.

If Bess Gideon was worried, there was no sign of it at lunch. She told Sarah that Kate had phoned; Harry Brendan was coming out for the weekend and Kate wanted them all for cocktails. Harry became, in Bess's telling, a belonging of Kate's which she was willing to share for an hour or two.

Even so, thought Sarah with a faint unreasonable pang which might well have come from Evelyn's inspiredly bad casserole, Harry would tell her the truth if he knew it. She was comfortably sure of it until she saw him that evening.

ix

"You know Rob," Kate Clemence had said half-wryly, and Bess: "Even Rob can wait five minutes . . ." Sarah saw the reason for both tones when she met Kate's brother at a little after six o'clock.

She caught only a fast glimpse of a bathrobed figure in the commotion of their entrance into the Clemences' living room. There were reminiscent shivers, the usual, "Isn't it cold?" and "The weather report said snow," and "Let me take your coat." Sarah caught Harry Brendan's glance with all the shock of the first time, and then she was being introduced to Rob Clemence.

She had gathered earlier that he was either an invalid or a convalescent, and the bathrobe and a faint tired limp that showed itself later bore that out. He was older than Kate, and startlingly fairer; his sandy hair curled crisply back from a high freckled forehead. Temper or pain had cut deep lines down his cheeks, disconcertingly like scars; and although he was obviously pleased to see the Gideons, Sarah would not have been surprised if the angular jaw had tensed suddenly, and something more than temper flashed out. He was the tightest, tautest man she had ever met.

He gave Sarah a rapid-head-to-toe glance that came back to settle on her face. "Well, well," he said with a lift of sandy-tufted brows. "What can Charles have been thinking of?"

The crudity of it made Sarah catch her breath. He was no taller than she, so she was able to keep her gaze level while she said coolly, "When, Mr. Clemence?" and someone—Milo?—gave a small titter. A hand touched her wrist and Harry Brendan, his face unfamiliarly dark, said lightly, "Where I come from we ask a girl what she'd like to drink."

Rob Clemence bowed slightly. "Then I beg your pardon, too. Kate tells me my manners are abominable, Mrs. Trafton, and there might just be a grain of truth in it. What'll it be?"

He expected her to say, "Nothing, thank you," and be put in the position of a sulky, party-spoiling child. "Rye, please, if you have it," said Sarah, and moved away with every appearance of calm.

Kate produced crackers and cubes of cheddar cheese; Hunter, his face thunderous, went out to help Rob Clemence with drinks. Talk built gradually up around the raised town taxes, an actress with a summer home here who had taken her third overdose of sleeping pills, and then, with a jump, the missile program. Under it all, Sarah held her anger as carefully as a match that might go out in the wind.

Bess had known she would walk into this; so, from his instant reaction, had Milo. And what was it, exactly? A verdict against her in the matter of Charles's death, or merely the resentment and license of speech allowed an invalid?

Rob Clemence himself settled it, or seemed to, when he leaned for a moment or two beside her chair. He said abruptly, "Ever broken a hip? It's hell while it's mending. Just when you think you can stop toddling around like an ancient it kicks you in the teeth all over again. I used to be a commercial airlines pilot, and here I am shuffling around in my slippers."

This was an olive branch, better take it. "Did you crash?"

"In a car," said Rob Clemence, dangerously sunny. "There was one of those famous little old ladies, the ones that drive only on Sunday, in the other one, and she's as fit as a fiddle. I'll be on the watch for her next time."

He winced a little as he moved away, but to Sarah's unforgiving eye it looked like a contrived wince. People in pain or under medical care had liberties denied to the rest of society; they could be as rude as they pleased and not be held accountable. It must, she thought, be a difficult privilege to relinquish.

Her empty glass was taken suddenly out of her hand. Hunter stood above her, looking down, his face at once brusque and bothered. "Are you all right?"

"Fine," said Sarah up at him, "perfectly happy," and only realized when he had left with her glass that she sat alone.

Milo had carried his drink to a window and stood with his back to the room, gazing out. Rob Clemence was like a ticking time bomb as he listened to something that Evelyn was confiding lengthily into his ear. Bess turned the pages of an expensive and beautiful book on archeology; Kate and Harry Brendan sat a little apart, contemplating their drinks, talking quietly now and then. When Evelyn interrupted herself to say alarmedly, "You don't mean to tell me it's seven o'clock? Oh, I must go over and look at the chowder," Sarah rose quickly.

"I'm nearest—can't I? What do I do?"

"But you don't want to . . . Well," said Evelyn, giving

in happily, "you could add the diced potatoes and a dash of thyme and then turn it down to low. But I really don't know why you should have to—"

It had begun to snow, the ground was already a faint crisp white. Sarah walked through the cold as though it were a decontamination room, across the Clemences' lawn, through the lilac hedge, into the long slope of darkness that the farmhouse lights didn't reach. It was a pretty, twinkling snow, as much silver as white in the glow from the kitchen window.

The chowder bubbled loudly on the stove, the only sound in the quiet house. Sarah added the potatoes as instructed and began a search through the spice cupboard for the thyme. Bottles seemed to topple as soon as her hand approached them, knocking over other containers. Why—a pause here to clean up some spilled parsley flakes—did she suddenly feel so nervous and disorganized? Surely not because of a scrap of conversation overheard only minutes ago: Rob Clemence saying to Bess in an undertone, " . . . think you're wrong. People like Peck have no rules, and they think we're suckers because we have."

And Bess answering fragmentarily, "—all very well, but what would you have done?"

Peck, believed for a time to have been a murderer; Peck, staring in through the kitchen window. Sarah turned her head helplessly, looked out at whitening branches of lilac beyond the steamy panes, and tipped the can of thyme.

The kitchen door opened very quietly. As it swung in Sarah thought wildly that she mustn't scream; she had read a hundred times that screams triggered fear and set off violence. But some sort of sound emerged from her throat as the door came open, and after a look of total astonishment

Harry Brendan walked up and took her simply into his arms, thyme and all.

It began as reassurance—"Who did you think it was?" "That man, that horrible Peck"—and turned gradually into a shaken kiss that quieted and held and grew stormy again. Harry said muffledly, "That's what I didn't do when I left you in New York," and Sarah, with the kitchen growing up around her, said in an equally obscured voice, "The chowder's boiling over."

She moved away and took off the lid unsteadily and turned the heat down; mingled with the extraordinary lightness of body and mind was the warning memory of Bess's voice: Harry and Kate . . . Harry and Kate.

Behind her Harry said with an odd violence, "I think we deserve a drink," and went to get ice cubes.

"We ought to be going back."

"But we aren't," said Harry. "Who will take care of this motherless chowder if we don't?" He switched on the light in the little pantry between kitchen and dining room, and the caged crow said obediently, "Hi, Milo," and sank back to sleep in a ruffle of feathers.

"Now," said Harry, planting drinks on the kitchen table, "what's going on? You look like a ghost, and it can't be only Evelyn's cooking. You're more than a match for Milo. Is it Hunter? Bess?"

Quietly, not tasting her drink but turning the icy round of it with one hand, Sarah told him. She held nothing back—that seemed impossible at the moment—and when she had finished Harry gave his dark head a shake as though he had just emerged from water.

"No wonder you look . . . Well, let's see. For one thing,

Nina was so distantly related to Rob and Kate, and even then by marriage, that I don't think Charles ever connected them in his mind. He was thirty when his father married Nina, and she was thirty-six."

The chowder muttered in another world. "It was one of those idyllic May-and-December affairs, or maybe June and November, that outsiders never quite believe in," said Harry. "Edward Trafton was a very odd guy, and he'd been lonely and bitter for years. Nina changed all that, and at the same time she was close enough to Charles's age to understand him, too. He'd never seen his father happy before, and at least he had that to hang on to after the heart attack. He and Nina were closer than ever then, so that when she died—"

His voice had been gradually slowing; it stopped in a trailing way, as if he had forgotten that he was speaking and even that Sarah was there at all. The glass she hadn't lifted was cold and wet inside her hand, and she was holding it much too tightly. She said with a peculiar feeling of trespass, "Did she die of pneumonia?" and Harry Brendan's gaze swung up and struck her like a slap.

"No," he said.

Sarah stood up and walked unseeingly to the sink, and after a few seconds of thunderous silence Harry's even voice began again.

Nina Trafton had been understandably vain about her beautiful hair; she had been painted a number of times with it hanging rich and loose. After three weeks of illness and fever—she had refused to be removed to a hospital—she was as illogical as a child about insisting that it be washed. She had actually gotten out of bed once, and crashed light-headedly into a doorway, cutting her forehead.

On an afternoon in February, with the house briefly emptied of everyone except the nurse, she had succeeded. Weakened by fever and drugs, warned by the doctor of the seriousness of a relapse, she had nevertheless gone into the bathroom, clad only in her nightgown, and moved a high stool into position before the basin. She had pinned a towel about her throat and stood a bottle of shampoo on the glass shelf and filled the basin. She had bent her head with its long tangle of fever-dulled gold, and struck the faucet so sharply that her head went into the water and stayed there.

Sarah hadn't turned from the sink; she felt incapable of moving. Milo had painted Nina ready to wash her hair—and how frightful that was, it gave him a new and ugly dimension. No wonder Bess had caught that knife-like breath when his bedroom door creaked open to show the easel. Sarah said into the stretched-out silence, "Where was the nurse all this time?"

"Asleep," said Harry Brendan shortly. "She said later that her tea had been drugged, but the laundryman who stopped at the house that day saw her moving around upstairs."

Sarah did turn at that, incredulously. With this frightening affair so recently behind them, all these people had shaken their heads blankly over Miss Braceway's murder and wondered what could have been bothering Charles. She felt as though she had landed in a gathering of well-behaved maniacs, who persisted in thinking that the cobra in their midst was a garter snake, until Harry went on.

Someone had had the presence of mind to preserve Miss

Braceway's teacup—the tea set to steep for her punctually at one o'clock every day and left on the stove—and the dregs were tea and nothing else. As her relief had not arrived the night before, she had been on duty an unbroken twenty-four hours. What more natural than to take a look at her patient, who pretended to be asleep, and lie down herself for a few minutes of badly needed rest? The times involved didn't agree with the laundryman's account, but the curtains in two of the upstairs rooms were straight-hanging white net, and the draughts that old houses were full of might have set one of them stirring so that it looked, to a casual glance from the lawn, like a moving uniform.

After the first shock, no one blamed the nurse. Her record was impeccable, she had exhausted herself in caring for her patient, and although she was familiar with the irrationality of fever and female vanity, she hadn't bargained on Nina Trafton's obsession. As a professional woman whose reputation was her living, it wasn't surprising that she clung to her story of having been drugged; as far as that went, Nina was easily capable of it.

"I'm afraid I've drunk your drink up," said Harry, light with an effort. "Say that six times fast."

"Milo painted Nina that way, getting ready to wash her hair."

"Milo—?" Harry's forehead wrinkled and then cleared. "I know she'd sat for him a couple of times before she got sick—she liked being painted with her hair loose and Milo fancies himself as an artist. I suppose he couldn't resist a dramatic touch later, or maybe he wanted to imply an attachment. Although for that matter I think every man who ever met Nina was a little in love with her at one time or another."

Of course; no wonder even talking about this had made him white. Sarah went to the stove and gazed blindly at the chowder, which rewarded her with a scalding burst of steam. She said before she could stop herself, "That must have made it nice for her husband."

The stillness behind her was absolute. Not quite daring to turn her head, not trusting either Harry or herself, she said, "Tell Evelyn, will you, that I'm putting in the rolls?" and after a long moment the kitchen door closed with furious calm and she was alone in the house.

So the subject Charles had kept locked up so tightly was still not to be examined, no matter what her own necessity. Never mind that Miss Braceway was dead, and Charles. Where Nina Trafton was concerned, you might look but you mustn't touch.

Sarah set the oven to heat for the rolls, thinking remotely that Evelyn, left to herself, would have inserted currant jelly and sour cream or some other unlikely mess. Whatever else Harry Brendan had done in that disturbing interlude, he had exorcised Peck. When she looked at the steamy windowpanes she saw Nina instead as Milo had painted her, stiff and out of drawing but with the surprising life that a child can sometimes produce with crayons.

Towel at her throat, Harry had said, but Sarah didn't remember a towel. Maybe Milo had left it out for aesthetic reasons, or maybe it was there in folds of—white, would it be?

Having gone that far, she was lost. Slipping into other people's bedrooms was hardly the best guest behavior, but then that was a rule not strictly observed in this house. Sarah went rapidly through the house and up the stairs to the door of Milo's room, as nerved to this as though it represented the blackest kind of danger instead of the embarrassment of being caught.

And there was Nina seated on the backless white stool, brilliant head poised eternally over the basin that had killed her. She wore a puff-sleeved nightgown of pale blue, and there was no towel about her throat. Milo had evidently had second thoughts about his portrait since the morning, because at the right edge of the canvas, close to the top, something in the blue background had been painted out in a sharp, noticeable patch of green.

Sarah reached for the wall-switch with a lightning hand. Her overstrained ears manufactured a sound of returning voices, and for one queerly terrified second she was afraid that she would reach the top of the stairs and find a man's face waiting furiously for her at the bottom. Milo's, stripped of spite and secrets, or Hunter's, the eyes gone like ice, or Rob Clemence's, his temper let off its leash and bounding up to meet her.

But there was no one there at all; there was no one in the house until safe moments later, and by that time Sarah had the rolls in and was closing the oven door. Evelyn, coming in ahead of the others, thanked her volubly, tasted the chowder and began dropping things into it. Sarah was speechless, even when Evelyn said chattily, "What would you say to a few cloves?"

Whatever had been painted out of Milo's portrait, or painted in and then obliterated, had occupied a space behind and a little above Nina Trafton's head.

X

PECK DID NOT COME the next morning, although the chicken house and pheasant pens awaited their regular Saturday cleaning. Sarah suspected that Bess was glad, in spite of the extra work it meant; it gave her a chance to demonstrate that farm life was not all a matter of open fires and pristine snow and beautiful idle birds.

She said crossly, "How that man does drink, and always the night before you need him most. I don't wonder that Hopkins fired him," but the grumble was unconvincing. She made a great play of getting into her outdoor clothes, bundling up, Sarah thought interestedly, as though she were setting out for Little America instead of twenty yards beyond the barn. The heavy boots and gauntleted gloves and woolen scarf were all intended to say, "This is what you'd have to do all winter if you lived here, and how would you like that?"

Milo had assessed the situation early and disappeared. To the dentist, he said; he was unruffled by Hunter's dry compliment on his bravery in having stood such a painful tooth all the day before. Sarah said after breakfast, "Isn't there something I can help with? Can I carry in the pheasants' water jugs, or bring out feed?"

Bess cast a significant glance at her lilac tweed suit. "Now, Sarah. Hardly."

"I have an old coat here," said Sarah suddenly, remembering it for the first time. "A raincoat I used to leave for weekends. If someone has a pair of boots I could borrow—"

Her feet were instantly assessed, with unflatteringly doubtful glances. Hunter said without a trace of a smile, "If you really want to go out, and you wear some heavy socks under them, I have a pair that might stay on you."

"Coat?" said Bess blankly. "Where, Sarah?"

"Upstairs in the guest room closet. Don't bother, I'll get it; I have to go up anyway."

"But there's all that furniture in the way. Hunter—"

He had already gone. Bess said briskly, "Better have some more coffee while it's hot, Sarah," and Sarah said with equal briskness, "I'd love some when I come down," and walked rapidly through the dining room and up the little back stair. Quick as she was, Hunter had been quicker. When she shot back the bolt on her side of the guest room door and opened it as though she would save him the trouble of looking for the coat, he was standing at the closed closet door with it over his arm.

It was a very old raincoat, badly in need of cleaning, and the sight of it gave her an unexpected pang; she had worn it last on that final weekend here with Charles. A petal of green silk scarf escaped from one pocket, and he had said that the color of it made her eyes as green as leaves.

Her face must have altered, because Hunter, toweringly tall and restless in this enclosed place, took an abrupt step toward her. "Sarah—?"

Bess's voice reached crisply up the stairs. "Hunter? Did you find Sarah's coat?"

Hunter looked goaded and annoyed at his mother for the first time since Sarah had met him. He called back that he had and she waited, but if there had been a moment when he was going to tell her something it was gone.

For some reason, perhaps because he had always kept so brusquely to himself, Sarah had never thought of Hunter as a source of information. It had come as a shock to her that he knew, from that unexpected question in the car, exactly what she was about here. Charles had never said much about him, but she had put that down to the fact that men took each other more for granted than women did, or perhaps there just wasn't much to say. Now she wondered.

Bess was at the far side of the barn, collecting quail eggs like a croupier from the tiered cages that were built shallow so that the quail, who flew straight up at the slightest alarm, could not gain enough momentum to knock themselves senseless. She said over her shoulder that she had put the feeders in the stable; Sarah could fill those with turkey pellets and, in this cold, add a sprinkle of corn. Bess herself would replace the feeders; she didn't trust the Silver with strangers, or even the Reeves.

Reeves . . .

Sarah took her time with the turkey pellets, examining these three enclosed pens with a more careful eye than before. They had originally been stalls, and the small windows high up under the slanting roof left the rear part in shadow except for the white snow-light that streamed through the small exists to the outside runs. At the moment, the only tenant in occupancy was the mild ungainly Silver hen, hiding from her warlike mate and listening hopefully to the rattle of the turkey pellets.

Bess had stood the water-holders in a row to be thawed at leisure as the pheasants would eat the fresh-fallen snow. With the feeders also out, the pens were empty except for the Reeves'; this held a propped hickory branch where they could roost and dispose their sweeping tails without damage. That left only the long, narrow nesting boxes and the litter covering the planked floor, but the nesting boxes were cleaned regularly and the litter swept out and replaced from the bale in the corner. So that whatever Charles had thought was here—the thing so important that he had broken a self-imposed rule by writing a private memo in his office engagement book—could hardly be here any longer.

Or could it? Was it coincidence that two of the three names had been the doubtful-tempered breeds which Bess insisted on caring for herself? The illegibly crossed-out name might have been Amherst or Copper; on the other hand it might have been Silver, which would confine his interest to the stable area.

What had Hunter said about the Silvers in the car driving home? "A tremendous wing span, and spurs like knives . . . Long John had lost his bit."

How big Long John was, three times the size of the Amherst cock, twice the size of the Reeves. The Manchurians seemed to wear their weight comfortably; Long John's was all power and alertness. Sarah's eye left him and went probingly around the stable. There was a medicine cabinet nailed to the wall above the bale of litter, and it held surprisingly human remedies: Argyrol, alcohol, sterile cotton, a tube of antiseptic, cod-liver oil, antibiotic tablets.

"It's pretty much kill or cure with pheasants," said Bess's

even voice directly behind her. "We've been quite lucky so far, nothing more than a frozen toe or an infected eye now and then. Thanks for doing the feeders, but hadn't you better go in and warm up? You look frozen yourself."

Sarah wasn't frozen, only unaccountably chilled at that brisk reasonable "kill or cure." In the corner behind the bale of litter stood Milo's mink-killing stick, business end up; from nowhere came the horrifying thought that if this were summer that darkened spot on the wood would have been clotted with flies. The mink's body had disappeared . . . and where was Peck?

("People like Peck have no rules, and they think we're suckers because we have." That was Rob Clemence's voice in a short sharp indictment, with Bess's emerging after it: ". . . what would you have done?")

"I think I will go in and get some coffee," said Sarah; she had begun, actively, to shiver. "Won't you, too, or can I bring you out some?"

"Oh, no. I'm used to this, but then," said Bess, delicately triumphant, "after all these years I ought to be."

In the kitchen, so spotlessly cleaned after breakfast that not so much as a spoon showed, Evelyn said sufferingly, "Oh, no trouble at all. I'll just—" and began to assemble an army of implements.

Sarah glanced into one of the flung-open cabinets. "Isn't that instant coffee?" Over Evelyn's protests and insistent taking-apart of the newly washed percolator she put on water to boil and spooned the powdered coffee into a cup. She said while she waited, "Does Peck do this often?"

Evelyn, putting the percolator away again, dropped the glass top with a clatter. She said, "Oh dear. Milo says he's always waiting for the day when I'll be all fingers. Yes, Peck's done it before; that's why he lost his job at the mink farm. The trouble is that about once a month he seems to—" Evelyn flexed her blue gaze at Sarah, preparing the way for a witticism "—drink up his pay."

"But then doesn't somebody call to say he isn't coming?"

"His wife does and says he has a touch of flu. Milo says that's short for under the influence."

"Milo is certainly droll," said Sarah, watching with wonderment Milo's daily victim. "Such a quick tongue. Did Peck's wife call this morning?"

"She must have," said Evelyn practically. "Or maybe he didn't even come home and she thinks he's here. You can't tell with people like that, can you?"

"People like that." "People like Peck." Peck was employed by the Gideons, then, out of the direst necessity. Knowing Bess, Sarah could not quite swallow Evelyn's earlier suggestion of philanthropy because Charles had been sorry for the man. Kill or cure was Bess's nutshell philosophy, and there was no room for faltering or sentiment. Somehow, Peck had been in a position to force the Gideons to hire him when he was released from jail.

And where did prescience come from? Coffee downed too quickly on a fluttering stomach, a conviction of something dangerous hidden here, a glance at a heavy blood-darkened stick?

Peck is dead, thought Sarah. She tried it quickly and irresistibly on her mind, like a child mounting to a forbidden height, and just as the child found out that it could balance there after all in spite of the stuffy warnings from its elders, she knew quite certainly that Peck was dead.

Hunter had almost finished cleaning the chicken house when she went out. The old litter had been piled in a cart to be added to the compost heap; he had only to line the nesting boxes with fresh hay. The Silkies rocked about with their mixture of swagger and trust, and Midnight came up to plant herself demandingly on Sarah's boot.

"I hope," said Hunter with barely restrained violence, "that the dentist had to pull Milo's tooth, and that it was quite deep-rooted."

All the way down to his toes, thought Sarah, bending to give corn to the fluffy little black hen. "Is this usually Milo's job?"

Hunter uttered a bark of laughter. "It's Peck's job," he said dryly, "and failing that mine or Bess's. Never Milo's."

He turned to swear briskly at the Silkie rooster, who had suddenly fancied danger to one of the hens and rushed forward with a ridiculous air of menace. The bantam held his ground, stance implying that if the broody hen were disturbed he would tear Hunter to pieces. Hunter by-passed the nest; he was almost done now, and Sarah had still not said what she had come to say.

"Your mother is certainly patient with Peck, isn't she?" Even his name seemed subtly dangerous now, but she managed it carelessly.

"It's an obligation of sorts," said Hunter after an instant of total stillness. His strong light-eyed face bent down and away from her, intent upon the distribution of dry sweet hay. "Bess repeated something to the police that the nurse had told her, about having been accosted by a strange man when she was walking in the field here one day. That's what put them onto Peck in the first place."

"Accosted?" said Sarah, her brows going up involuntarily.

"Miss Braceway's word, I take it. I suppose he shouted, or said something she took for an improper suggestion. At any rate she told Bess, and Bess told the police, that the man had come from the direction of a hut at the back of the mink farm. So . . ." Hunter shrugged. "It seemed to add up to Peck, particularly as he'd been in trouble with the police before."

How very suitable Peck was in every respect for the role of brutal killer, and what a nuisance for the Gideons that he had not only been freed but was in a position to demand work from them. Only why work, why not just money? Peck didn't sound like a man to worry inordinately about the devil and idle hands.

He would have been furious at being arrested on Bess's hearsay statement, particularly if—this went shockedly through Sarah's mind—it were pure invention. Miss Braceway had complained of being drugged at the time of Nina Trafton's death. Bess wouldn't want that issue brought to light again after all these months, and what better diversion for the police than Peck, already known to be a dubious character?

Peck was a countryman, and shrewd; he might very well have argued to himself that the Gideons, wilfully implicating him in the murder of the nurse, had something to hide. The fact that Bess hired him on demand would seem to him proof, and he would be emboldened. And he had access to the pheasant pens. . . .

Hunter stood the hayfork in the corner, surveyed his handiwork, and reached for the door latch. He said over his shoulder, "Has it occurred to you, Sarah, that if you keep on with this you might find out something about Charles that you won't like?"

Sarah had thought herself too single-minded to be surprised into anger by anything these people might say to her, but Hunter's cool curious tone caught her off guard even while her mind registered the openness of the jump from Peck to Miss Braceway to Charles. "You mean," she said with careful distinctness, "something I'll like even less than the fact that after six weeks of marriage to me Charles jumped out of a window? Frankly, no, it had not occurred to me. And while we're on the subject, did you have a lunch date with Charles that day?"

Hunter, who had opened the door to let in a flutter of white light and biting cold, closed it again, turning a face of almost musical-comedy astonishment. "Lunch date?" he repeated. "In New York?" His tone removed New York to the distance of Hong Kong. "No. What on earth put that into your head?"

"I just wondered."

Hunter's expression changed. He held the door for her without a word and Sarah walked by him, more shaken by that brief glance than by anything he could have said.

He might have lied to her only moments ago, but could he have contrived that look of pity?

Charles had not killed Miss Braceway, she assured herself, rushing at this particular fence in the refuge of her room. Putting everything else aside, he had been in New York at the time, so that she had not, in spite of Hunter's frighteningly off-hand suggestion, lived with and slept beside a man capable of battering a woman's head and face so viciously that identification had to be made through other means.

Was it the obvious thing, then—a physical fear of Sarah

after that chance incident on the bluff? Dr. Vollmer had blunted that spear, but it still hurt surprisingly. Sarah tried to reconcile Charles's nightmares with the possibility that he had confided the subject of them to his family, but she could not. In any case, no matter what the state of his mind, he could not have confused her with a Reeves or an Elliot pheasant.

There was one other area to explore, and she had to force herself to do it as though she were opening the door of a dark and dangerous room. Harry Brendan had indicated it in that curiously remembering voice when he said about Nina Trafton: "Every man who ever met her was a little in love with her at one time or another."

Did it all lie there, the key to the whole business? Consider Nina, married to an embittered man almost twice her age, acquiring in the process a tall good-looking stepson only a few years younger than she. Consider Charles, for that matter, gentle, rather shy, coming into sudden contact with all that ripe and smiling warmth.

Suppose—but what unpleasant work it was—some escapade of theirs had precipitated Nina's illness? Charles had not had a nature for involvements, much less forbidden ones; his conscience would have punished him tooth and nail.

Sarah found herself staring with a trance-like blankness at the floor. How convenient if Charles had kept a journal of some sort, but he hadn't, only a small red leather book that contained the addresses and telephone numbers of friends and nothing more. It had no lock, although at some time or other she had seen exactly the kind of key that would fit a diary. She had held the key in her hand, wondering idly at the smallness of it. She had been sitting on a bed, as she was now . . . Sarah put out her hand, palm up, and bent her head, using her body to trick her mind.

And it worked, the other background was suddenly there. It was the day after Charles's death, and her blood had been pounding savagely at the base of her skull in the type of headache that aspirin couldn't touch. Irrationally, she had been unable to stand the sight of Charles's suits hanging there so tidily in the bedroom closet, and although someone had suggested tactfully that she ought to empty the pockets first she had swept the suits from their hangers and folded them frantically into two big suitcases.

She had repented of that later. Suppose, after the bags were locked away in the basement, that the lawyer should want something, or Charles's office? When Bess had told her firmly that she must lie down, she had walked docilely into the bedroom, closed the door behind her, and gone through the pockets of the suits. There was no reason why the housewifely action should have seemed so frightful to her, but it did; she felt as surreptitious as a thief, and she didn't even want to look closely at the little pile that accumulated on the bedspread.

The tiny key caught her eye, the only one, she realized now, that was loose. There were some neatly folded papers and a few cards too, and at length she found a blank envelope and slid everything into that and put it—

Memory balked there. In a bureau drawer? No, because her search for the snapshot of Charles hadn't turned up the envelope. In one of her own suitcases?

Her idly determined search, all this time later, found it in her small dark blue suitcase. Sarah emptied the envelope onto the bed. The diminutive key was there but it was a hollow victory, like having been right about the population of Tulsa in some given year; all it proved was an accurate memory. The business cards held unfamiliar names, the folded letters were a receipted bill, a note from somebody about stock shares, and a doubled-over envelope containing the cancelled part of Pullman tickets to Chicago and back on December first and second.

Both were early morning trains—and somewhere there had been a tremendous mistake. According to Dr. Vollmer, Charles had kept an appointment with him on the late afternoon of December first. According to the scribbled pasteboard in her hand, Charles had been in Chicago at the time, exactly as he had told her.

It had to be a clerical error in Vollmer's office, because otherwise Charles had never been to a psychiatrist at all, and it was some other man who had given his name and his background and said that Charles Trafton went in mortal fear of his wife.

XI

Below Sarah, like shock made audible, the telephone rang. It rang twice more before a man's stride crossed the dining room and Hunter's voice said in the abruptly challenging tone with which he always answered, "Hello?"

There was a pause while he listened and Sarah listened, too, with a queer and automatic detachment. "No," said Hunter. "No, we haven't . . . Let's see, I think it was Thursday night . . . Yes, we certainly will."

Mrs. Peck, thought Sarah in that curiously removed way, beginning to worry about her vagabond spouse, wondering at the length of this particular spree. Coming for answers to —of all people—the Gideons.

Her mind went chasing fugitively after Peck's wife, like a guilty child trying to change the subject; it refused, just for the moment, to admit the enormity of what it had discovered. Because if someone had run the risk of posing as Charles at the psychiatrist's not once but three times, it could only have been to establish a record of mental imbalance. And that in turn would have to mean—

Make sure of it first, whatever her own frightful certainty.

Sarah moved at last, transferring the tiny key and train checks to the zippered compartment of her purse, returning the envelope to a pocket of her suitcase. Why had she never noticed before that the suitcase was only a little bigger than Bess's travelling case, navy calf instead of dark green alligator, but easily confused in an uncertain light?

But everything looked different to her now, even her own drained and sharpened face. It was like having read the end of a book in advance, so that every minor incident was colored, every character—now that you knew—invested with his own destiny.

Mechanically, Sarah went into the guest bath and washed her face in very cold water, chiefly because something had to be done to it before she went downstairs. Lipstick helped, and a faint touch of the rouge she almost never used. She was combing her hair before the dim mirror in her own room when doors began to open and close, voices lifted, someone below her—Bess?—said, "I don't know. I'll ask her," and began to walk toward the back stair.

Sarah was out of her room in a twinkling, although she could not have explained her unwillingness to be approached there. Bess met her in the dining room doorway. "Oh, Sarah. Harry and Kate are driving into town, and want to know if you have any errands for them."

"Or if you'd like to come," said Harry Brendan; after one rapid glance at Sarah's face he turned away, as if to divert attention from it.

"Of course," said Kate Clemence after a tiny lag. She stood against the dining room fireplace, dressed in the clothes that suited her best: gray ski jacket, its hood back, impeccably tapered gray ski pants that set off her long legs. Her ragged dark hair looked brilliantly black by contrast, so did the brows over the great gray eyes. "Preston isn't what you might call a shopping center—but I keep forgetting that you know the town."

So you do, thought Sarah. She said to an imaginary third person between Harry and Kate, "If you don't mind an extra passenger, I would like to come," and went to get her coat.

She came back to find them congregated in the kitchen: Evelyn stirring something at the stove, Bess sorting quail eggs for shipping, Harry Brendan leaning against the sink and gazing with exasperation at Kate, who sat at the kitchen table with an air of permanence. She had taken off her jacket. She said to Harry, not turning her head as Sarah entered, "No, really, I'd rather. I had nothing pressing to do anyway, and frankly I've gotten so comfortable here . . . Do you think I could have a drink, Bess, in honor of its being Saturday?"

The last had a faintly driven air, like a wisp of steam escaping from under a clamped-down lid. In the car, Sarah said without expression, "Did Charles know she was in love with him, do you suppose?"

Harry backed clear of the gatepost. "They were unofficially engaged at one point." After a short pause she could feel his glance swing to her silent profile and away again. "Years ago. Long before you came on the scene."

. . . And what else, Sarah wondered astoundedly, might Charles not have bothered to tell her? Sunny, open, clear-as-a-book Charles . . . well, in a way it served her right. It bordered on arrogance to presume that anybody at all was that uncomplicated. Or had there been something about the breaking-off with Kate Clemence that made it a matter of ethics with him not to mention it?

She said after another string of telephone poles had gone

by, "What happened?" and saw Harry Brendan's hand lift from the steering wheel and then drop back. "Nothing," he said, but his voice sounded different, puzzled. "It just dwindled off."

"About the time of his father's marriage to Nina Clemence."

Harry swung the car in at the snowy curb in front of one of the shops and turned to face her. He said in what sounded like an indictment, "Sarah, you were fond enough of Charles to marry him. Do you realize what you're trying to prove?"

The strap of her calf handbag, holding what it held, seemed to burn across Sarah's wrist. "Yes," she said, and got out of the car.

The drugstore's phone booth was occupied. Sarah bought cigarettes, equipping herself with quarters and dimes, and walked half a block to a street booth. After an interval of long-distance queries and clickings and coins rattling out of the chute and having to be deposited again, she was connected with Dr. Vollmer's office in New York.

It was either a bad connection or the waiting room was being redecorated with a power drill. After a good deal of repetition on both sides, Dr. Vollmer's absence at a convention was established, and—would Mrs. Trafton hold on a minute—the fact that Mr. Trafton had come in for his last appointment on December first. Of course there was no possibility of error, their records were most accurate. In fact, that had been Dr. Vollmer's mother's birthday and he had been particularly anxious to leave the office on time. (Aha, mother complex, Doctor?) The nurse remembered quite clearly that as an earlier patient had delayed him, Dr. Vollmer had had to shorten Mr. Trafton's alloted hour by fifteen minutes.

And there it was. Sarah had thought she was sure before, but all at once her forced detachment shattered like glass; she had to clench her free hand to keep it from shaking. She said through the rushing in her ears, "What did Mr. Trafton look like?"

The far-off voice said angrily, "Just one moment. Who *is* this speaking, please?" The operator came on, requesting more coins; Sarah cried, "Wait! Please—" and her unsteady fingers sent her neatly-spread change rattling off the shelf. Someone tapped metallically on the glass door of the booth, and she turned her head distractedly to see Milo Gideon smiling blandly at her and holding up a quarter.

Sarah hung up the receiver without a word. She gathered her gloves and purse and opened the door, feeling the icy air in every pore of her damp body; to bend and search for her scattered change was, for the moment, beyond her.

Milo did that, puffing exaggeratedly, straightening to say chidingly, "Tsk tsk. Easy come, easy go. Here you are." He dropped the coins into her hand and tipped his round head to one side, studying her brightly. "Evelyn was monopolizing the phone at home, I take it, because Bess isn't that mean about the phone bill. I happened to see Harry's car there as I came out of the dentist's, and somehow I thought I might find you. Do you know that tooth of mine is so inflamed the dentist can't do anything with it yet?"

Sarah would not be subjected to an intimate view of Milo's mouth, which seemed imminent. She said rapidly, "How awful," and somehow Milo stood directly in the path of the step she started to take away.

"It promises to be my Operation," he said mournfully,

but his owlish face, without changing a single plump line, had grown as cold and sharp as ice. "What did you think of my portrait of Nina, by the way?"

So it had not been all imagination, that brush of panic she had felt at the doorway of his room the night before. Milo had come back from the Clemences' before the others, and looked in through a ground-floor window and seen the light there—or, thought Sarah steadyingly, Bess had told him about the earlier and accidental view.

A boy bicycled past them on the sidewalk, a woman went by with a baby carriage and two small children who besought her for pennies: "We won't buy gum-balls, honest, Ma." Sarah didn't answer Milo directly, but then he didn't expect her to. "Why did you paint her that way?"

"Whimsy," said Milo after a second. It struck her that he was horribly like his crow—or had the crow picked up from its master the tipped head, the round and mocking stare, the air of secret malice? "I'm as whimsical as all get-out," said Milo. "But it makes you think, doesn't it?"

"Drink it," said Harry Brendan authoritatively, "or I will, and the last state of this man will be worse than the first. *Sarah.*"

Time seemed to have rolled back, Sarah thought, lifting her glass obediently; this was Harry as he had been in the frightful interval after Charles's funeral, bending her to his mood, knowing instinctively what she needed, cutting off the dangerous withdrawal.

Charles's death had been shocking and inexplicable then; it was at once simpler and more shocking now that it was murder. There was no other logical conclusion to arrive at: no one would bother to set the stage for suicide, no one would have to. Nor, in setting the stage, plant the victim's wife as a cause of actual fear, a bone to be thrown to some assiduous detective who might question the suicide of a man in Charles's position. An ace in the hole.

What Sarah kept seeing was almost invisible—the hair of blue fibre from the dining alcove curtain caught under Charles's fingernail. Not in the last-second change of heart the policeman had suggested, but in a struggle for his life. Because he had been pushed from the window, thrust out, beaten away from the sill.

Impossible not to think about what must have led up to that. A telephone call, probably, to make sure that Charles was alone. Charles opening the apartment door to someone he trusted, making drinks; betraying, to this sympathetic and deadly face, something he mustn't be allowed to repeat. The window in the dining alcove being raised, Charles—because there were no indications of a struggle—being summoned there on some casual pretext. ("Isn't that Sarah now, at the corner?")

How had it felt to be toppling from a killing height, to reach out in a last frantic effort for an anchor and feel only the graze of cloth? Almost everybody knew how it felt in nightmare; Charles must have had a second, or seconds, to know how real it was.

That was what had turned Sarah's stomach upside down. She forced herself to go back to the drugstore and buy what had to be bought, and when Harry Brendan came back to the car she was sitting in it very quietly, not crying but swallowing steadily and convulsively.

If he was surprised, he hadn't showed it. He had sensibly opened both front windows of the car and, not so sensibly, put his arm around her and held her firmly. He had said a lot of disconnected things, alternately brisk and soothing, ending up with, "Well, you can't go back to the house like this. Oddly enough, neither can I. Let's have several drinks, shall we?"

He was very quiet about it, but Sarah felt suddenly ashamed because he had known Charles much better and longer than she had, over a matter of years. Now, when she had put her glass down, he said, "Are you going to tell Bess about all this?"

Bess. Hunter Gideon might have gone to Dr. Vollmer, or Rob Clemence, or even Milo. Psychiatrists did not, from Sarah's hearsay acquaintance with them, demand birth certificates nor any other document; a medical history might be taken but you were who you said you were. (Even, for the time being, Napoleon.)

"No," said Sarah, "not yet." Harry did not appear to have noticed the small package she had carried from the car. "Did you have a lunch date with Charles that day?"

He didn't ask what day. "No. I got the night train down when Bess called me."

Out of her own shock and bewilderment, Sarah had not telephoned Bess until midnight; she could still remember the long empty drawl on the line while she waited for the ringing to wake someone. That had allowed time for whoever had killed Charles to get back to Boston by plane, and from there to Preston by car.

The check came. Sarah opened her purse to put her cigarettes away, and the tiny key, nestled with the cancelled train checks inside the zippered compartment, seemed to clank at her. She said, "Did Nina Trafton keep a diary?"

Harry's gaze shot up from his drink. "Indeed she did. Edward Trafton was a bird-watcher and an amateur botanist and a do-it-yourself weatherman all rolled into one, and Nina kept his field journal. The barometer went down so many points, crocuses came up ahead of schedule, cedar waxwings were observed at the bird feeder. Heady stuff. I imagine it's still in the house somewhere. All set? Don't forget your package."

The diary wasn't significant, then. On the other hand, why keep a key to a nature log? But it mightn't be the key of a diary at all, it might have fitted a jewel box or some special drawer; it might even, thought Sarah, suddenly flat, have something to do with Charles's office, although it would be odd if someone hadn't come looking for it before this.

She said briefly, picking up the package, "It's a camera."

". . . Oh. Yes, I see. From what you've seen of this Vollmer, do you think," said Harry in a neutral way, "that he's going to admit he was taken for a ride?"

Sarah stared back at him, shaken. "But he'd have to. Besides, he'd be furious at being used like that; he'd want to get back at whoever did it."

"And get his name in the papers in connection with a homicide investigation, if the police see it the way you do . . . Well, maybe."

"The way I do? But there's no other way to see it," said Sarah incredulously. Some of the sick coldness she had felt in the car came back; it was, in a curious way, reflected on Harry's narrow tightened face.

He wasn't looking at her, but at the table top. "It's been three months. Granted that someone could know in advance that Vollmer would be out of the way when Charles died—"

"That's not so terribly hard," said Sarah, quiet with an effort. "If you mark off a certain section of the city, and call every psychiatrist in it with a request for weekly appointments, one of them will turn out to be going on a winter vacation, particularly around Christmas, or off to a convention or somewhere."

"All right, let that go. It's still been three months and we'll presume," said Harry, still not looking at her, "that a lot of people go in and out of Vollmer's office, and he had no reason to be especially interested in that one patient at the time. Suppose he made an honest mistake, or just plain couldn't remember? The police might put you down as an overwrought widow wanting to get out from under."

"Not with the railroad tickets to prove Charles wasn't even in New York that day."

"He could conceivably have gotten those from someone else."

Sarah stood up, sweeping gloves and handbag and camera into a heedless bundle. She said softly and unbelievingly, "You don't want to find out, do you?"

"Me," said Harry musingly, "or Hunter or Milo or Rob Clemence." He smiled up at her without humor. "Yes, I suppose I do. But if the police start digging into it, they are going to go one hell of a long way back."

"Back to Nina Trafton, you mean."

"That's what I mean," said Harry, matching her tone exactly. "I think it's eminently possible that Charles killed Nina, and that the whole thing is going to make a twenty-four carat mess."

XII

So THIS WAS what Hunter had meant, this was why he had given her that queer compassionate glance.

In the car, Harry said gently, "Sarah, I'm sorry. I'd much rather not have told you, but it's—something you'll have to take into consideration."

"Oh, it is, isn't it?" said Sarah light-headedly. "You must all have been very relieved when Charles decided to marry. Marriage is so steadying; it weeds out those bad little bachelor habits. But you couldn't be a witness at the last minute, could you, Harry? You begged off, which shows—which shows . . ."

"I begged off, as you call it, because I found out that I couldn't stand watching you being married to anybody at all," said Harry shortly. "And before you go off into a tailspin, you ought to know a little of the background. For one thing, I'm sure Charles had no intention of killing her beforehand, for another, it was quite—understandable. Nina Trafton . . ."

Sarah had told herself numbly that she wouldn't listen, but she did. Edward Trafton emerged again, bitter and lonely, a constant reproach to Charles, who after all had his own life to live. Into this bleak personal landscape, on a chance visit to distant relatives she had just discovered she had, came Nina Clemence, ripe and warm as a peach, mature enough for poise and discretion. Her warmth, her mixture of deference and independence, perhaps most of all the fact of a childhood made difficult by extreme poverty, had captivated Charles's father.

After their marriage, she had taken the reins of the household from Bess and managed—to everybody's surprise—expertly. The butcher was enslaved, and reserved special cuts of meat. The laundry, never counted by Bess, came back with its full complement of shirts and sheets and pillowcases. Nina liked gardening, and the house began to bloom with flowers. Edward Trafton was a different man.

Largely because of the change in his father, Charles had idolized his stepmother. He could now pursue his own concerns without worry, and Nina, of his own generation, was there to talk to when he wanted. She flirted just enough to flatter her elderly husband—with Milo, with Harry, with Rob Clemence, even, unavailingly, with Hunter—but that was as natural to her as her walk or smile or beautiful heavy hair. But her real attention was for Edward: she went on long expeditions, no matter what the weather, to dig up a rare fern, or log a scarlet tanager out of season. The diary she kept was really a record of success for a marriage that mightn't have been expected to succeed.

And all of it had been a mockery.

Harry Brendan didn't know how Charles had found out, nor to what extent it went. Charles, coming to him, had been incoherent with shock and rage and, although he couldn't put it into words, disillusionment and hurt pride.

Nina had been laughing at all of them, all along. She had been carrying on an affair or affairs, bringing home, straight-facedly, a lady's-slipper or Bixton's fern after her assignation in the woods, basking in her husband's approbation while she looked forward to the next secret meeting. It even seemed possible that she had enjoyed the game as much as the candle.

Harry had tried to cool Charles's dangerous rage, had pointed out that if the object had been to make his father happy, Nina had succeeded, had said when that argument failed, "Wait. If you're thinking of contesting the will, you've got to have proof. Or talk to Nina. Chances are she'll take a smaller settlement and get out."

But Nina Trafton had contracted pneumonia by then, and either because of her illness or because she had asked for protection, the nurse would not let Charles see her.

"There are ways around that," Charles had said grimly.

And Miss Braceway, whose tea steeped so handily on the stove every day at an appointed hour, had been drugged on the day of Nina's death—only it was a little more complicated than death, it was murder.

Sarah realized that Harry's voice had stopped moments ago; did he possibly think he could leave it here, come this far and no farther? Her own voice sounded tiny and flat to her, the way it did in a theater lobby between the acts. "Where was everybody that day?"

At a local game-bird show, Harry told her, held every year by a group of fanciers who bought or traded birds with an eye to the coming breeding season. Normally only Bess and Charles and Kate Clemence went, but this time Nina's illness, with the resultant tiptoeing and worrying and staying close to the house until she seemed to be out of danger, had given it the air of a dazzling social occasion. Even Hunter had gone, and Rob Clemence.

Sarah knew what had to come next: the fact that the show was held in a huge auction barn, that people came and went constantly; that, with babies being hoisted on their parents' shoulders for a better view, cocks crowing militantly at each other, the wild beat of wings and crowding around as a bird was removed from its cage for point-by-point inspection, it was impossible to know where any one person was at a given time.

"Well then," said Sarah instantly.

Harry didn't inquire into that or even glance at her; he kept his eyes immovably on the road. "Charles came to me afterwards. He said, 'I never meant to kill her, I swear it. I only wanted to let her know we weren't the fools she'd taken us for, and tell her to get out.' "

And Charles had said exactly that, Sarah knew it from the very expressionlessness with which Harry repeated it. The words weren't so much said as pronounced. They built up a convincing scene, of Charles confronting Nina while the nurse slept in that heavy drugged sleep (there would have been two cups of tea, of course, the innocent one left); of Nina thanking him mockingly for the opportunity of washing her hair and going ahead, maddeningly, with the preparations for that.

How vulnerable she would have looked then, this woman to whom his father had left the farm and the major part of his estate, with her back turned and her head bent over the basin. So sure of herself, even knowing from his face why Charles had come, that she paid more attention to the feminine task she was bent on than to the man behind her.

Actual harm mightn't have been intended at all, the angry

thrust at her head the equivalent of a slap delivered in a moment of unthinking rage . . . No, thought Sarah, suddenly and completely sure. Charles might have done it to a man, but never to a woman. He could never, under the pressure of any rage, have left any woman with her face toppled drowningly into a basin of water under the weight of her hair.

Someone had done just that. Not Charles, although he had cleared the killer's path—and was that where the nightmares came from? "I don't care what he told you," Sarah said clearly. "I will never believe that Charles killed his stepmother. Drugged the nurse—yes. The rest of it—no."

The corner of her eye caught the quick embattled half-turn of Harry's head, as though he would have liked to agree or even disagree with her and couldn't quite bring himself to do either. The car rounded the corner that would take them to the house. Sarah said challengingly, "Besides, on the basis that Charles did kill Nina, who killed Miss Braceway? You're not going to sug—"

Without warning, and with a roughness that caught her in mid-word, Harry slewed the car in to the side of the road and stopped it. His face was tenser than Sarah had ever seen it, and his eyes darker. "If you think I like any of this one damn bit better than you do—" he began, and paused with an air of weariness, as though the task of explaining was mountainous but he would tackle it anyway. Sarah shrank a little from the thoroughness of his direct stare.

"I'm not that much older, but Charles was like a kid brother," he said abruptly. "Very young, in spots. As intolerant as an adolescent in his judgments. He never made allowances for human frailties in anyone—not even in himself. He always had to put haloes on the people he liked. I could have told him that sooner or later Nina's was going to fall off with a bang. It wouldn't have helped, but still I could have told him. How do you think I felt when it did, and she died, and Charles began walking around like a guilty secret on legs? How do you think I felt—Old Friend Harry—when he walked up to me with you on his arm? My God, how do you think I feel right now when we've got to exhume him like this?"

Sarah felt violently buffeted. She said to her hands, "I'm sorry," realizing all over again that Harry had known Charles much better than she, possibly better than his family; that the things in Charles that had come as a surprise to her—the strength that wasn't there, for instance, had been known to Harry all along and hadn't affected his liking in the least.

She said, "I didn't mean—"

"Neither did I." Unpredictably, he was smiling at her, but there was something a little wry in the smile. "Miss Braceway . . . Well, six months had gone by, remember, and she must have worked on a lot of other cases. And she was insatiably curious; she'd have had to be to go prowling into that shack on the mink farm. Maybe there was some drunk holed up in there, maybe some poor guy had stashed away everything he had in the world and came back and found her—"

He shrugged and started the motor. Sarah said, aware and not caring that she must seem to him like the drip of water on stone, "All right. That takes care of Miss Braceway. Who hunted up a psychiatrist in our neighborhood—one who was going abroad shortly—and went to him and pretended to be Charles? Who killed Charles?"

The rail fence and the sign that said "Pheasant Pharm"—that would be Milo's work—came into view around a curve. Harry Brendan said very soberly, "Are you absolutely sure anybody did, Sarah?"

It took a moment for her unbelieving ears to sort that out. "But the train checks—I showed you—and it *was* the same date, the nurse . . ."

Something stopped her, and her voice trailed off. Harry swung the car into the driveway and braked it before the barn. He said almost lightly, not looking at her, "How did you manage to get Charles onto a train?"

And this was it, this was at the bottom of the oddness in him, the parrying. Charles had hated trains with a hearty, almost a holy hatred. There was nothing mysterious or neurotic about it; he hated the dirt, the noise, the food, the service, the inevitable delays. Fortunately his job required almost no travelling, and when it did he flew. So that when Harry Brendan had seen the train checks he had thought—what?

It was impossible to be angry when her own mind had to grope for the answer. Sarah said concentratingly, "It was—wait, it was right after that terrible crash on take-off in Chicago. I had a touch of flu and I was very unreasonable about everything, especially Charles's flying at just that point, so in the end he agreed to go by train."

And said, smiling at her in one of the unguarded moments that had become so rare between them, "I hope you know that I wouldn't do this for anybody else." For some reason the memory was knifing. When Sarah lifted her head from an unseeing study of her hands, Harry said slowly, "He would have. Yes, I see."

His voice was calm, but his face had changed indefinably.

The reluctance had gone out of it, and the careful reserve. The glance with which he swept the length of the house was as brilliant and measuring as though there were a face at each window. "In that case," he said, "I'd better have the train checks. Not now, later, and as publicly as possible."

The house seemed different to Sarah when they went in; her new certainty of Charles's murder, and Nina's, chilled and darkened it.

Evelyn reflected the changed atmosphere, greeting them at the door with a hushed and important gravity. Hunter rose, loomed briefly, and said, "Get you a drink," but again that hardly scratched the surface of the silence. Even before he opened the door to the dining room, showing a slice of pale yellow wall and window and Bess at the telephone with her back turned, Sarah realized that all of them—Milo, Kate, Rob—had the self-consciously preoccupied air of people overhearing something.

There wasn't much to overhear. It was a conversation so one-sided that even Bess's single syllables were cut off. She said, "Yes, of cou—" and, "I know how you must fee—" and, "If there's anyth—" and a peculiar tension built up in the living room.

After a wordless eyebrows-up glance around the room, Harry Brendan had joined the ranks and was studying a framed pen-and-ink as though it had just been hung. Milo, stretched on his spine, peered at a Chinese puzzle that glittered in his short soft hands; the faint repeated clicking of metal brought him oath-like glances from Rob Clemence, tight jaw set, on the couch opposite. Kate sat at a window and gazed at the lawn with a rapt unconscious air that was undone by her strained and rigid throat muscles.

Sarah lit a cigarette she didn't want and listened to the infectiously quickened pace of her own pulse and drew in the glass ashtray with the burned match. It was a habit of suspended thought, but this time it didn't produce the usual random designs. Secretly, horrifyingly, the match in her fingers formed a "P" and then an "E" and a "C"—

The receiver went down and Bess came in, face shocked, short gray curls wilder than usual because she was pushing blankly at them with a leather-gloved hand. She said unbelievingly, "That was Mrs. Peck. The police just called and told her he's—Peck's dead."

Nobody moved. In that lightning interval Sarah had erased the letters in her ashtray, so that only a small shining square remained, but it was too late to help Peck.

"He'd been drinking all day, it seems, and he must have stumbled on his way home and hit his head on a rock in that brook near their house," said Bess more strongly. "It was so cold last night, and the brook was deeper than usual after all the snow we've had. They think he died of exposure."

And you could hardly, thought Sarah, tensely not looking at Harry Brendan, put it more clearly than that.

xiii

LUNCH WAS a kind of rite for Peck's memory, in which not everybody joined. Food was deferred by common consent in favor of another drink; even Evelyn, who sipped at sherry only on state occasions, seemed grateful for hers. It was Rob Clemence, freckles showing more than usual on the tight graven face under the crisp curling hair, who said with mordant amusement, "I'm a little confused here; can somebody fill me in? This morning Peck was an absentee nuisance, a known drunk, and, if everybody present will pardon me, a surly son-of-a-bitch. Why are we all wagging our chins like this? Is he changed?"

"Considerably," said Harry Brendan dryly.

"Oh, biologically, yes. Don't," said Rob, turning almost clairvoyantly upon Evelyn, "quote *De mortuis* at me. Anybody who has to be dead to get a good word—"

"Rob," said Kate almost pleadingly, and he stopped with a shrug.

Evelyn hadn't been about to quote anything at anybody, Sarah thought, watching the other woman curiously. Sudden death was a topic which ought to have set her off on a marathon of other sudden deaths she had known or read about, but instead she sat wrapped in a silence of her own, lashes down over—what? But then what had it been on the night of Sarah's arrival, when Evelyn had first spoken about Peck? Pleasure, triumph, some secret and malicious excitement?

Milo had followed the direction of Sarah's gaze and slid his glasses down, observing his wife over them. "Cat's got her tongue," he said blandly to Sarah. "Nice pussy."

Evelyn smiled absently without looking up; for Sarah the smile had a spine-prickling quality and she glanced hastily away.

The others were talking about Peck and what poor Mrs. Peck would do now. ("Heave a great sigh of relief," said Rob roundly.) It was true that Peck had lost jobs as fast as he got them, but there was always work to be had in the country, and whatever else his faults, Peck had been wise in the way of birds and animals. Mrs. Peck, evidently a woman of strong character, had managed to extract enough of his pay to keep them in food before he went off on his periodic benders. The wonder was that he hadn't smashed his car into a tree or come to some other violent end long before this.

Sarah listened and was almost lulled. Drunks did not require pushing; they fell of their own accord, and the soaking in the brook combined with the bitter cold would have done the rest. It was all very predictable for Peck, it fitted him as exactly as the murder of the nurse.

"I wonder," said Evelyn almost apologetically, "where he got the money?"

There was a pause, and a focussing of attention unusual for Evelyn's utterances. Then Hunter said shortly and gloomily, "He'd just been paid."

"But that was Thursday night, wasn't it?" The bright blue gaze held only an innocent wish for enlightenment. "And if he'd been drinking all that evening, and all yesterday— I mean, Peck usually went through his pay faster than that, didn't he?"

A calculation of dollars and cents travelled silently around the room. Rob said sardonically, "Now that we've all discovered what a sterling character he was, I suppose I'd better not say that he mightn't have been too particular about where his money came from."

The subject had grown acutely uncomfortable. Perhaps to change it, Kate Clemence said, "What happened to your hand, Bess?"

"My . . . ? Oh, this." Bess moved her right hand with a recollected air, showing a stab-like cut, short but vicious, in the flesh between thumb and index finger. "Long John. He's always had a bad temper and he's getting worse, although I do think someone's been teasing him. Those Elwell children, probably. They're absolute devils."

"And he's never liked his new pen, has he? I suspect that he's quite an age and set in his ways," Kate said thoughtfully. "When he calms down you might put the pair of them in one of the outside pens. The Manchurians would probably like—"

Sarah didn't hear what the Manchurians would like; the moving of the Silver pheasants was a signal her mind stopped at and stayed with. When had that taken place? Had Charles, when he wrote down "Reeves" and "Elliot", put the Silvers in the same ill-tempered category, and then crossed out the name because at that time they were in an outdoor pen that held no place for concealment?

It would make quite a difficulty, if you had hidden something in a pen occupied by tame and docile pheasants—the Lady Amhersts, say—to find it presided over by a trumpeting and militant Silver. At most seasons of the year the Silver would not molest Bess, the source of his food and water and raisins and tomatoes; now, with the breeding season not far off, he would harm any intruder and probably damage himself in the process.

It was a safeguard, in a way, for something you didn't dare leave in the house, in case of a search. (But why keep it at all, whatever it was? Why not destroy it?) On the other hand, a delicate balance had been achieved here. Four deaths had been laid variously to accident, suicide, and random violence, and whoever had been responsible for them would not want the balance upset. Say that X had hidden something incriminating in one of the pheasant pens—because it was something that couldn't be destroyed easily and there wasn't time after murdering Nina Trafton? Because the laundry truck had stopped and X had fled in a panic? —and, after all these safe and lulling months, along came Sarah, rebelling against the motives for Charles's suicide, intent on examining the background.

X would now want to get rid of the tangible object that Charles had known about or deduced, but a distinctive stab on the hand, combined with a breaking of the proud snowy tail feathers and a disturbance of the stable planks, would mark his progress all the way. The hairline division between coincidence and a related plan would be fatally crossed.

And what had Bess just said about the Silver? "Somebody's been teasing him."

Bess had a cut on her hand.

". . . Sarah?" It was Harry Brendan, whose preoccupied silence during lunch had gone unremarked because he was apt to be like that and, a virtual stranger to Peck, not really qualified to speak. "Before I forget, did you ever find that memo of Charles's for me? He said he'd written it down on the stub of something or other." "Business," explained Harry in an aside to Bess. "A well-feathered bird in Brookline."

"I don't know," said Sarah, and although this had been prepared between them in the car, as had the envelope she took from her bag, her voice sounded to her hollow and overdone, something out of an amateur play. "I'm afraid I forgot, but I did gather up all the stubs and tickets and cards there were. Do you suppose it might be somewhere in here?"

The room listened and watched as the envelope changed hands. "Thanks, it might be," said Harry, and dropped the envelope carelessly into a pocket and consulted his watch. "Where was it you had to be at three o'clock, Kate? . . ."

Sarah went up to her room, avoiding Bess's expectant eye; once she had agreed to sell the farm, any pretext for lingering would be over. Her mind followed Harry Brendan, driving somewhere with Kate beside him; tranquil, quiet equal-to-anything Kate with her disarmingly ragged and shiny dark hair, her white throat, her gray eyes that were big enough to float in.

Sarah stood in front of the mirror and assessed herself in a blank but careful way, thinking that if that was what Harry wanted, she couldn't compete. She didn't look tranquil at all; she looked pale and driven and uneven-tempered, someone whom Harry might have felt so sorry for that he had put his arms around her out of compassion.

Below her, the house was quiet. Moving quietly and carefully, unbothered by conscience, she shot the little bolt on her side of the guest room door and turned the knob and let herself in.

One of the twin beds was still pushed against the closet door, as it had been when Hunter confronted her with her raincoat over his arm, and a slipper chair had been placed on top of the bed. Wallpaper stirred around her feet as she crossed the floor, lifted the chair down, listened for any sound that might filter up through the iron-lace hot-air register, and began to move the bed.

It wasn't heavy, and it needed only pivoting. The closet held a collection of wire hangers, two plastic bags of summer clothing, and on an upper shelf a number of what appeared to be account books.

They were. Sarah glanced at random entries: "$350 for garden tractor. Hurricane damage to chicken house, $75. Quail eggs shipped, May to July, 100 doz."

Tucked in among the pages of another one were carbon copies of arrangements for land to be plowed, hay fields to be re-seeded, and one strip of land, going northerly some four thousand feet, bounded by etc., etc., to be sold to the addressee.

There was no date, no heading beyond Dear Sir, and of course no signature. It took Sarah some time to realize that the Gideon property, long land-bound, was or had been in process of being unlocked.

What value would that add to the property, with the new highway into the South Shore? Beyond eye range, the farm comprised at least fifteen or twenty acres, and what were building lots worth per acre? Was this what she hadn't been allowed to go near, was this why Bess had sent Hunter so urgently up to this closet to get Sarah's forgotten raincoat?

There was another book of some kind, frosted with dust. Sarah reached for it, fingertips identifying the smooth calf even before she lifted it down. It was a pretty little dark-blue volume, its pages gilt-edged. Protruding from the miniature lock was a duplicate of the tiny key in Sarah's handbag.

"Gale winds last night, edge of hurricane," Nina Trafton had written in a rapid curling hand. "Called tree warden to see if split old cherry can be saved. Two bird feeders smashed, must replace . . ."

And on another page, "First frost. Pretty to look at when the sun came up but a death sentence for our poor asters. Orchards will be deserted now as their tenants go south . . ."

Orchards? What orchards?

Sarah went on leafing through the pages. There were more references to the weather and nature in general, and a lengthy description of bird calls at dawn. "What bird is it that sings under my window like two knives being sharpened against each other?"

My window.

The only name that occurred, and that at infrequent intervals, was Edward Trafton's. Even then he had a dragged-in-by-the-heels sound: "Edward says it will soon be time to mulch the strawberries. Ours are the Cranford variety, very small, but making up in color and delicacy of flavor what they lack in size." "Edward saw a ruby-throated hummingbird this morning."

The feeling grew on Sarah that this had not been so much written as copied out of a country-correspondence column in a newspaper, with Edward's name thrown in for verisimilitude. Even granted a devouring interest in nature, would any woman as ripely attractive as Nina Trafton have been as selfless as this in a diary meant only for her eyes? Would any woman at all—particularly a woman living in a house with her husband's relatives—have made no personal references anywhere in the diary? It seemed a contradiction in terms.

On the other hand, if she had been observed in the keeping of a diary, and someone were curious enough to take a look at it, he would reap only comments about mulch and humming-birds and wind velocity for his pains.

And there was the matter of the extra key. A spare, in case one got lost? Possibly, but Charles would hardly have kept it in that case. He would certainly have kept it, knowing what he did about Nina, if he had found it in a suggestive place after her death and arrived at the obvious answer: two keys, two diaries. The other one the exact mate of this in everything but content, so that Nina could confide in it openly, even amusedly.

It wouldn't burn easily or unobtrusively, not with the lock and the triangles of brass that cornered the blue calf binding, but it mustn't turn up to undo the innocent look of Nina Trafton's life and death. . . .

Sarah paced her room until she remembered that every footstep could be heard by anyone in the dining room below, and sat chainedly down on her bed. She had to remind herself that another diary was purely imaginary—but the key wasn't, nor that notation of Charles's on the day he died, nor the nightmares.

Nor was the woman herself. Every word, every glance, every small detail that related to Nina Trafton increased

Sarah's conviction that she had been the victim of some uncontrolled love or hate or jealousy; that she had died simply because she was Nina. She had thought she could balance a tightrope, walking delicately among these various personalities and enjoying the risk, and she hadn't made it after all.

Sarah was queerly sorry for her, because whatever else she was she had been warmly alive, and whatever else she had done she had made Edward Trafton perfectly and innocently happy. Even now, after all these months and by a total stranger, she had to be shaken consciously free of, like a beguiling dream.

Looked at in one light—the fact that Charles had indeed drugged Miss Braceway and gone to Nina but left her alive, perhaps in her bedroom, perhaps coolly gathering her towel and shampoo—the nightmares made a sensible pattern. He would have blamed himself for her death, which must have come as a tremendous shock in spite of his bitterness, but the tragedy for which he had set the scene was simply that—until the murder of the nurse. Sarah could still remember his whitened face on the late summer afternoon when Kate had told him. His inescapable conclusion then would have been that Miss Braceway, doggedly defending her own reputation, had remembered or suddenly been able to prove something that turned Nina's death into murder.

And it had to be one of the people among whom Charles lived who had known that the scene was being set, that the nurse would be unconscious and Nina, to all intents and purposes, alone. Someone in whom he had rashly confided, or who had overheard him confide in Harry Brendan, and watched him very carefully after that.

Peck's arrest had been a reprieve, because if the nurse had been the victim of a drunken and senseless violence, it didn't go back to Nina. Charles was still morally guilty, but he had not been an unwitting accomplice to murder.

With Peck's release, the black burden would have become, as all burdens put down even briefly, intolerable. He did not even have the relief of sharing it with his wife. Obsessed with his guilt, unable to forgive himself, he could not believe Sarah's judgment would be less damning than his own. He did not have the courage to face what he thought would be her inevitable rejection of him, although he knew that his silence was wrecking their relationship as surely as a confession would. His marriage was cracking up, he had alienated himself from his family and friends. He had lost any hope he might have had that time might solve his problems. He must have decided to come forward, at whatever cost to himself and one other member of that close little group, and he must have said so.

Memory prickled coldly at Sarah, presenting her with the day Charles had come home edged and driven, gaze unnaturally brilliant, mouth twisting with irony at her suggestion of a weekend at the farm. He had made himself an outsize drink with careless haste, but when he repeated his salutation it hadn't been careless at all but intent and downstaring. "*Here's how . . .*"

X—and what a frightening faceless sound that had—would have soothed him down, would have said, "Wait. Think of Sarah. It's her future too, you know, and besides, you can't be sure that the nurse's murder wasn't freak coincidence. Look here, I'll give the police up there a jog and get in touch with you."

Because although Charles's death sentence had been passed, it mustn't be executed until it could be explained away in character. (Like Nina's vain and reckless concern with her hair, like Peck's drunken stumbling into a brook —Peck, who had tended the pheasant pens.)

Three weeks had been allowed Charles, for three visits to a carefully selected psychiatrist and the laying of a trail to Sarah in case his suicide didn't pass muster. By plane, Boston was commuting distance from New York, and who in Preston was to know that X hadn't simply gone into Boston to do some Christmas shopping or attend a pre-holiday party?

They had been three weeks of growing strain for Charles at what he intended to reveal about himself and, unavoidably, Nina, so that Sarah had said yes, her husband had been markedly nervous of late; his office had said that Mr. Trafton had been most unlike himself. . . .

And whom had he had a luncheon appointment with, on the day he died? Kate Clemence.

Sarah hadn't a watch, and time had gone peculiarly astray for her, but there was still a faint warmth to the sunlight on the wet black boughs of the cherry tree. She hadn't loaded a camera since she was fourteen, but this particular make hadn't changed. She went downstairs for her coat; idly, like someone bent on capturing only the brilliance of the pheasants, she went outside.

XIV

THE REEVES and the Lady Amherst were dancing. Sarah had seen the courtship before, on weekends before her marriage, but it always held her still and amazed; it seemed a ritual you could only expect to observe after days of patient vigil in some secret part of a woods.

Both cocks, the Reeves in his cold gold satin-and-lace, the Amherst warmed by red and gold and shifting blue-green over his white breast, seemed to be demonstrating for each other as well as their bored and restless hens. They ran lightly and delicately for a few rapid steps, then the capes flared at once outward and upward to the very edge of the round and fiery eyes, while the brilliant bodies were tipped steeply on one leg for a full display of plumage. Each pause was accompanied by a hiss and a spreading of the gay fringing tail feathers. Both hens seemed to have urgent errands inside, but they were cut off by more short gliding runs and tips and flarings and hisses.

In the middle of the three runs that opened off the stable, the Silver watched with outrage. His shining black crest was erect, his red felt seemed to have extended so that he looked like an aroused chieftain dressed for war. In spite of the wire between them, Sarah took an instinctive step backward when he suddenly stood erect, grunting with anger, and began to beat his powerful snowy wings with a peculiar rushing and clicking sound.

"He's a devil, isn't he?" said Hunter admiringly at Sarah's side. "And look at old Trooper there. Not as romantic as he looks. Watch."

He extended a fragment of bread through the wire. The Amherst cock stopped in mid-dance, took the bread eagerly, waited to see if any more were to be had, and resumed his pirouetting. Sarah, waked out of her absorption, realized that with the loss of Peck everybody had been pressed into service. Milo was coming forward with an empty feeder, Bess had emerged from the Manchurians' pen with one of the big blue birds in a firm and expert grip.

She said worriedly to Hunter, "Where's all this eye trouble coming from? Get the Argyrol, will you, and some cotton and boric acid if it's there?"

The pheasant submitted to doctoring with an almost trance-like docility. Bess walked away with it, talking quietly and steadily, and Hunter looked at Sarah's camera. "Going to take some pictures?"

"I was," said Sarah carelessly, "but I don't know how fast this film is. I doubt if it could keep up with the Amherst."

"Bess had very good luck with a batch she took last spring. I'm sure she has an extra set somewhere."

Was this the automatic politeness it seemed, or a test? Sarah smiled at him. "I'd like to try my own luck," she said. "Would you have any more bread to entice him with?"

Hunter gave her a long level glance that she came close

to flushing under before he said pleasantly, "Yes, I have," and glanced around. "I think over here . . ."

The spot he led her to was perfect: sun slanting over her shoulder, the Amherst cock a fairy-tale bird against the dark snow-sifted pine boughs. Sarah moved the camera imperceptibly, under the guise of focussing, until the tiny glass aperture held Hunter's profile, sharp, vivid, alert. Something, the context or the gilding of light on his hair, gave him an elusive resemblance to Charles. She said over the camera, "I'm sorry to keep you; this thing seems to be—" and Hunter turned his face instinctively.

"—stuck," said Sarah, but the click of the shutter had been simultaneous with the sudden upward veer of his head.

"Jet," he said, getting to his feet and gazing briefly at the sky over Sarah's shoulder. "Did you get Trooper?"

"I think so." There had been a jet. She could still hear its diminishing scream, but the sky here was so full of them on weekends that they were almost a background noise. They were certainly no novelty to be stared at. "Thanks," said Sarah, cordial with an effort. "I'll see what I can do over here."

She pretended to photograph the Japanese Coppers, by far the most valuable birds on the place; the going price was something like two hundred dollars a pair, and that didn't include the price of importing them, maintaining them during the necessary period of quarantine on the West Coast, transporting them here. The corner of her eye saw Milo going on his reluctant rounds, circling closer to her like an inquisitive bee.

Sarah strolled unconcernedly toward the Manchurians' pen, worrying about the fading light, and was rewarded. Milo presented himself with a mock-offended air. "When do I get to have my picture taken? I'm in full color right now, believe it or not."

Wouldn't the man who had masqueraded as Charles realize the danger of a camera in Sarah's hands? Milo stationed himself at the side of the pen, and she realized with a little shock of triumph that he hadn't taken off his glasses. People who wore them usually did for this kind of photograph, because of the distorting glitter of light on the lenses. On the other hand, the owlishly round dark frames were the feature a stranger would remember about Milo's face.

Sarah said into the camera, "There's an awful lot of reflection from your glasses," and Milo's hand lifted and dropped again to his side. "Let's face it. I'm the intellectual type, and it's the pheasants you want anyway, isn't it? Say when, so I can take a manly breath."

Even then Sarah did not quite trust him. She said, "One second, while the hen comes a bit closer—" and quick as her finger had been on the shutter, Milo was quicker. Deliberately, he had made an elaborate face.

It was the kind of thing he would think amusing, and there was no excuse for the flash-fire of anger that took place inside Sarah; briefly, she could not trust herself to speak. Milo said something innocent about hoping she had done him justice, but she pretended not to hear.

Two pictures taken so far, one a blur of movement, the other a comic-strip grimace. They would have to be taken again, at random, and although they wouldn't be full-face they would have to do. The color would help. It would show Hunter's weathered complexion, Milo's dark hair and glasses, Rob Clemence's grooved, freckled tensity and sandy curls—if she could ever manage to entrap Rob.

It didn't, in Sarah's present black frame of mind, seem

very possible that she could. She passed the stable runs on her way back into the barn. The Amherst cock was still absorbed in his delicate enamelled dance, but the Reeves had dropped into a bored walk. The Silver followed Sarah inside as though he had read her mind.

If she were to explore the pens, it would have to be done at night, when the pheasants roosted so numbly that they were at the mercy of any marauder, because Sarah knew she could never face those beaks and spurs and rushing wings by daylight. A pheasant seemed a ridiculous thing to be afraid of, but there it was. Not the least of her fears was that one of them would fly straight at a window in a panic and drop at her feet with a broken neck.

Sarah had had her head turned, looking back at the dim planks under their covering of litter; just in time, she avoided colliding with Evelyn.

The other woman was unevenly flushed, face blotched with the red patches that appeared under strong emotion or contact with one of her—was it sixty-four?—allergens. She seldom ventured as far as the barn, because of the presence of the quail. She said briskly enough, "Someone's on the phone for Bess, and I was just running out, but I see she's busy. I'll tell them . . ."

She turned and went rapidly back into the passage that led to the kitchen—because the phone wasn't off the hook at all? She not only hadn't been running, she hadn't been moving at all; the precise and unconscious part of the ear that counts clock chimes told Sarah that Evelyn had simply been standing there.

She could have been lost in admiration of the quail on the other side of the barn, three crowded tiers of small speckled egg-factories, or been gazing down the ramp into the stable. Or she could have been watching through the barn window into the corral.

The window gave a view of all the far pens, and even a corner glimpse of the Amherst run. It would have shown Hunter, Sarah with her camera, Milo and his last-minute grimace. It would have caught Bess's rapid hardy walk as she went about tending her birds, and, Sarah noted, it afforded a glimpse of the Clemences' back yard through a ragged break in the pines.

Harry Brendan's car was back. So, presumably, was Kate.

The pheasant pens would have to wait until some still hour of the night. Kate Clemence, who had loved Charles, who had had a lunch date with him on the day he died, did not.

"Yes," said Kate, making tea in her immaculate kitchen. The door was closed, shutting out Rob and Harry Brendan and any kind of friendliness. "I was supposed to meet Charles that day, but as he couldn't make it there didn't seem much point in mentioning it. I didn't know you as well then, and I was afraid you might—" her mouth smiled pleasantly and candidly at Sarah "—misunderstand."

Two body blows, thought Sarah, smiling pleasantly and candidly back. The obvious one, and the implication that Sarah, even misunderstanding, wouldn't have cared.

She said in Kate's own tone, "How right you were. Brides aren't noted for their tolerance. Did Charles by any chance say why he didn't want it mentioned? It's an academic interest, I suppose."

Kate gazed at her and then back at the tea. "Lemon," she inquired, "or cream? No, I remember, you don't take anything. I'm sure you'd much rather have had a drink."

"There you're wrong," said Sarah. Her smile felt like a dagger between her teeth. "I'd much rather have tea. Did Charles say?"

"He said he was afraid," said Kate. It ought to have had a wrung and reluctant air, but it came out like everything else Kate said: calm, open, unruffled.

"Of what?"

"Don't you think," said Kate, "that you're putting yourself through this unnecessarily, Sarah?"

How kind and careful she was, and how solicitous of Sarah's feelings. Did she never blink? Perhaps she even slept like that, great gray eyes wide and serene, unperturbed by dreams. *The dreamer cometh.* Where had that sinister little phrase sprung from? Sarah said carefully, "Putting myself through what, Kate?"

Kate glanced down into her cup. "Charles had been drinking when he called me, I gather. That was something new as far as I was concerned, so perhaps I didn't make enough allowance for it. What he said was that his marriage had been a terrible mistake, and he had to tell somebody, but he was frightened of what you'd do if you found out."

"Such as . . . what?" said Sarah softly and fixedly; she couldn't help herself. "Leave him? Push him through a window in a fit of pique?" She walked the length of the kitchen and back again, fast. "Granted all this was true, what could you have done, I wonder?"

It was probably fortunate that the kitchen door opened just then, and Harry and Rob came in for drinks. Rob was complaining savagely about foreign policy; Harry, seeming to inhale the atmosphere between the two women, picked up Kate's tea and tipped it into the sink. "Did you know," he said seriously, "that an eminent chemist has succeeded in pickling rhinoceros tendons in that stuff? Whereas with Scotch the same tendons remained fresh and pliable."

He made Kate a drink and shepherded her out of the kitchen. It left Rob in charge of Sarah; he said dryly, after a lightning glance at her, "A little Scotch for your tendons?" and when she shook her head, "What was the girlish chat about?"

The question was light, something about the pause that followed it was not. "Charles, of course. It's a subject," said Sarah shortly, "that seems to be full of little surprises."

"Oh?" The bottle was tipped in the steady freckled hand; fascinated, Sarah watched a thin stream of liquor splash onto the counter top two inches away from the waiting glass. "For whom?"

"For me. That is, so far," said Sarah, and as Rob seemed unaware of the puddle of Scotch, picked up the sponge.

He took it from her without moving his sharp gray stare. His jaw had gone tight, making the very amiability of his voice dangerous. "So that's it, that's why you won't let Bess off the hook. You want to get out from under, no matter how. You're determined to dig up another reason why Charles went to a looney doctor."

Another reason. Harry Brendan was the only person she had told of even one, and he would not have gone around confiding it to people—would he? Or had he only pretended to believe her, because he was attracted to her and was waiting for this phobia to spend itself?

Sarah was still stinging with anger from what Kate had said; this new undermining thought undid her caution completely. She said curtly, picking up her bag, "I don't believe Charles ever went near a psychiatrist. I don't believe he jumped out of that window. And if you were about to warn me that if I keep on about this I might find out something worse, I've already been very thoroughly warned about my own good—and I don't believe that, either."

She could not, at just this moment, face either Harry or Kate. There was a back door and she started blindly for it. Behind her, Rob said in a mock-startled voice, "Look out, she bites!" and then, in a very different tone, "Maybe you've been warned about this, too, but don't you think that's a rather dangerous thing to go around saying, if you're right?"

He was squeezing the sponge out in a grip so tight that his hand looked contorted. "I'm right," Sarah said evenly, "and I suppose it is dangerous, in the proper quarter."

She had lost track of the time in this sharp and queerly vivid interval, and when she opened the door the dusk, holding steps and trees and shrubs in a watery uncertain grasp, came as a surprise. She turned as she went out, said pleasantly, "By the way, have you seen Milo's portrait of your cousin? That's a rather dangerous thing to go around painting," and closed the door very quietly behind her.

She didn't immediately go down the railed wooden steps. She looked back through the uncurtained window into the lighted kitchen, and Rob Clemence was still standing at the sink, sponge forgotten in that tendon-whitening grip. While she watched, he dropped it onto the drainboard, picked up his drink, and walked rapidly out of the kitchen. Sarah saw without surprise that he wasn't limping at all.

XV

Bess had undergone her usual six o'clock sea-change, short gray hair brushed high and crisp above her eloquent and rather haughty face, figure a spare black cut-out after the rough and careless clothes of the day. Sarah realized with a new awareness that Bess exaggerated both her existences, and enjoyed each because of the other. This metamorphosis was not the usual shower-and-change; it was a ritual.

Charles had called her, fondly, the Duchess of Pheasant Pharm. How had that inborn air of command subdued itself to Nina Trafton? How would Bess have felt if, after Edward Trafton's death, Nina had planned to sell the farm, and with it Bess's dual life?

The dusk had been navy blue when Sarah stepped out of it into the living room; the primrose light inside turned it to an instant black. And the stage had been set for a talk more formal than the earlier one in Bess's bedroom.

This was normally the hour for cocktails, but there was no sign of Hunter or Milo or Evelyn. The white door to the dining room was closed, and from behind it, over the gravelly protests of the crow, came the strains of a rhapsody on the record player. Music to Sell the Farm By, thought Sarah sardonically, but she was too tired and too bitter to care very much.

She said abruptly, "You were quite right, Bess. This is a lovely place, but I wouldn't have the faintest notion of how to hold it together from one day to the next."

"It is big." Bess was much too poised to show any easing of tension, any triumph at a mission accomplished; in a classic maneuver, she concealed the depth of her anxiety by an apparently open reference to it. "I won't pretend that I'm not delighted. I've gotten rather bound up here with all those foolish birds. But let's not talk business tonight. You aren't going to rush away now that you've decided, are you? You'll stay at least until Monday?"

Sarah nodded. Bess said with an air of keenness, "You're tired, aren't you, Sarah? And of course this can't have been the happiest place for you to come. . . ." She opened the dining-room door as impatiently as though she herself had not arranged the closing of it, and called crisply, "Hunter? You are making drinks, aren't you?"

Sarah went upstairs. She had a notion that she was going to be examined very thoroughly by someone's eyes during the next few hours, and she armored herself unconsciously.

She changed her suit for the only dress she had packed, navy tissue wool as slender and active as a fencer's costume. At her throat and ears she put the pearls that Charles had given her, and then instinctively took them off and wore only earrings, small pale-gold leaves that shone quietly against the short curve of her hair. Leaning toward the mirror, lipstick poised, she remembered without warning the context of the phrase that had jumped into her mind in Kate Clemence's kitchen.

"The dreamer cometh." It was from the story of Joseph and his brothers, which had haunted her as a child because, on a thundery summer afternoon, she had found a shirt of once-brilliant calico impaled on pussy willows in a field behind their house. And how did the rest of that infinite cynicism go? "Behold, the dreamer cometh. Come, let us kill him, and cast him into some old pit, and we will say: Some evil beast hath devoured him . . ."

Charles's dreams, evidence of his breaking-point. Come, let us kill him, and cast him— Sarah shivered once, uncontrollably, and turned her back on the mirror as though the cruelty lay there.

What had Charles wanted of Kate Clemence on that last day, so urgently that he had telephoned her in Preston? Sarah was quite sure that the "terrible mistake" Kate had quoted referred not to his marriage but to the drugging of the nurse. Everything sprang from that.

His sudden anxiety to talk to Kate suggested a new development of some kind. A suspicion of someone who had never crossed his mind before? He would know that he had been observed slipping away from the gamebird show to go back to the house and confront Nina; had he wanted to ask Kate—a neutral witness, not of his own family—who else had been missing from the show shortly afterward? Had he, in fact, needed the knowledge for a scheduled meeting, later, with the killer to whom he had so innocently betrayed himself all along?

Sarah rubbed at her tight and aching temples. What mattered more than anything else at the moment was the question of a diary in a pheasant pen, a pretty little dark-blue volume whose key, dropping from the lock and settling into some crevice in or near the stable, Charles had found and recognized and kept.

The necessity of finding it, of making solid sense out of the noted-down names of pheasants, was not a matter of abstract justice nor even, wholly, a desire to avenge Charles. It was simply the fact that Sarah could not go back to New York and take up her life again—and wonder, until the not-knowing made up her very existence, like a hole in a sculpture.

It struck her, as she went down the narrow little stair, that she was placed almost exactly as Charles had been.

"—still think he had something to do with all those mink," said Milo.

Hunter's formidable eyebrows went up, his gaze stayed on the rug. "He had no great reason to love us, if it comes to that."

Bess turned flashingly. She said, "What on earth do you—?" but Milo was there before her, head tipped to one side, preparing the way for a profundity. "People never love their employers. It's against nature. Do you find cats loving dogs? Worms getting up early?"

They were talking about Peck, inevitably, because Mrs. Peck had called during the course of the afternoon to say that the police had made a routine check of her husband's last hours. Although Peck had been inclined to belligerence when drinking, he had had no quarrels in Tod's Bar and Grill nor, later, in Eddie's Cafe. In fact, he had bought drinks for the house at Eddie's and, pressed to repeat this hospitable gesture, announced with decorum that he was late for his date with a rolling pin as it was. After a brief encounter with a glass door which he had presumed to be open air, he had started home alone and unassisted.

Cheerful, thought Sarah, studying her hands, because he thought there was more money where that came from. Never suspecting that he had been enticed into drunkenness, that his small demands, indicative of a larger knowledge or near-knowledge, had become intolerable. Certainly not looking for, and totally unable to cope with, the sudden thrust of hands in the cold quiet night.

". . . do you?" said Evelyn in Sarah's ear. "I said, you never have to diet, do you? It's wonderful the way some people don't."

Did she work at being inane, wondered Sarah blankly, or was it a gift? No ordinary intelligence could produce such observations as, "Where would people be without furnaces?" or "I knew a woman once whose husband was in the insurance business." (Pause, significant flexing of the round blue gaze, mysterious nod.) "There's a lot of money in it."

That was one Evelyn. Another sprang out occasionally, a sharp hard awareness that counted up the mockings and stored them carefully away. How had either Evelyn liked having her usefulness in the household wiped out by a young, efficient, radiantly pretty woman? Milo's habitual barbs would be much harder to take in that presence; watched, smiled over, Evelyn would have fumbled more than ever.

Violence could be born out of a thing like that, probably was, uncounted times per day, behind the innocent death certificates issued all over the world. It mightn't start out to be murder any more than a chance comment started out to be a blazing argument. But once it was done, there was no going back, and any subsequent killings would not take the name of murder either, but of self-preservation.

"I see you still wear your ring," said Evelyn in a confidential tone.

They both looked at the narrow band of platinum.

"Shouldn't I?" asked Sarah, trying hard for amiability. "Or is there a rule under the circumstances?"

"Oh no. It's just—" began Evelyn, and launched into the saga of a friend who had lost her husband in a fire, and although she was young and most attractive and had a tidy little sum of money in bonds, her men friends were put off by the fact that she continued to wear her wedding band. Whereas the truth was that she had put on weight and couldn't get the ring off. A woman should never let herself go, should she?

Sarah nodded and shook her head now and then, and thought how empty the room was without Harry Brendan —like food without salt, or a cigarette without a match. He was over at the Clemences' now, parrying Rob's incivilities, teasing Kate, sitting close to all that handsome calm. He would forget Sarah. He would find her, if he should remember her, by comparison small and ill-tempered.

How was it possible to ache like a sophomore at the very thought of Harry and Kate? It was Bess who had first bracketed their names together as an accepted thing—and perhaps it was; they had known each other for years, they had Charles in common, Harry himself was the knotty kind of problem that would afford great scope for Kate's special talents. Old loyalties generally won out over new attractions, however startling and strong.

Sarah became aware that Evelyn's low confiding voice had stopped. She said mechanically, "How awful," and Evelyn gave her an astounded look. "To have married all those oil wells? Frankly, I think it was the best thing she could have done."

Dinner, coffee, the dishes afterward over Evelyn's automatic protest. For the first time Sarah was acutely aware of the total blackness of the country night at the windows, unbroken by light or any sound other than an occasional mournful brush of wind around the chimneys. All the birds —Midnight, the pheasants who would break the dawn with their high metallic shrieks, the bantam rooster who would answer with an eagle-sized crowing—were asleep in their feathers, fed and watered and protected through another day.

Presumably even Long John slept, hoarding his grievances until morning—but how very black it was going to be in the stable, how startling the ray of the flashlight that hung from the wall of the passageway to the barn. I won't think about it now, thought Sarah, and instantly her mind began to embroider the stable floor with rats, clawing secretly about for corn or turkey pellets or even an unwary pheasant. Long John had killed a rat once, drilling a savage hole in the ugly gray head. . . .

"Do you feel all right?" asked Evelyn curiously, and Sarah said yes, putting away the dish she had been wiping in blank circles. She wanted to know, nonchalantly, if Bess ever had any trouble with rats, and Evelyn gave a little shudder. "Peck kept them down with poison, because of course wherever there's feed . . . He found a rat-hole in one of the stable pens once, but he stopped that up. Anyway they wouldn't come in the daytime," said Evelyn, turning to give Sarah a reassuring glance. "Only at night."

However casual she had seemed, Bess had obviously marked this as an occasion to celebrate. Before Sarah had a chance to follow Evelyn out of the kitchen, while the red rubber gloves were still subsiding after being blown into, Hunter appeared in the doorway with a tray holding Bess's treasured liqueur glasses, stemless little bubbles of pale clear yellow, their etched leaves studded with tiny painted flowers. "Benedictine? Brandy? Or a mixture?"

He had Bess's ability to look as natural with the delicate glasses as he did with a hayfork. "Brandy, please."

Hunter switched on the light above the liquor cabinet in the wall opposite the crow's cage. The crow said, "Awk, hi, Milo," in an irritable mutter and went back to sleep. Hunter added bottles to the tray; he said without looking at Sarah, "You're satisfied about Charles, then."

It was still somehow a shock that this brusque remoteness had looked so sharply and exactly into her mind. "Satisfied doesn't seem to be quite the word," Sarah said with care. "I've learned about Nina, if that's what you mean."

"He wasn't to blame. Neither of them was," said Hunter astonishingly. "It was on the cards from the beginning. Charles was impressionable, Nina . . ." He shrugged. "This isn't the Victorian age. Nobody but Charles would have made such a mountain of it."

Did he really believe what he was saying, Sarah wondered amazedly, or did he only intend her to think that he did? Charles was impressionable, he had said—and what about Hunter? He hadn't gotten those knowledgeable eyes, nor the subtle lines of experience at their corners, from nowhere. And a startling softness, even an idealism, often lay under just this kind of no-nonsense coating. Hunter turned suddenly and caught her inspecting gaze, and for a moment he did not seem remote at all.

In the living room Sarah sipped her brandy, listened idly while the others talked, responded when Bess asked her tactfully about her plans. She said that she might go away for a while, she had always wanted to see the Southwest, but that she would probably end up at an advertising agency again. It was the only job she knew, and she would have to work at something; she couldn't simply settle down and do nothing all day. It seemed at once real and unreal as she said it, like a needed operation for which the date had not yet been set.

Predictably, Milo began to hum the "Serenade to a Wealthy Widow." Bess stopped him with a glance. Time seemed to have stalled, as though everybody knew exactly what was in Sarah's mind, until Evelyn said with a patient air, "Can I take these glasses out now? I don't know about anybody else, but I'm asleep on my feet."

"Not your feet, precisely," said Milo, peering across at her, but all at once sleep was in the air. The wind seemed louder and colder, the night blacker, beds inviting, the very lamplight exhausted. Bess told Sarah to have a good sleep. Milo touched his jaw reflectively and said he would take some aspirin up with him. Hunter stayed in the dining room, hand on the light switch, until Sarah had mounted the stairs to the attic room.

The house settled into darkness. Water gushed through the pipes and died into silence, footsteps ceased, doors closed with finality. Sarah turned her own bedside lamp off and smoked four cigarettes, carefully spaced, before she put on her flat and soundless slippers, eased her door open, and tiptoed down into blackness.

XVI

EVEN AT THE DOORWAY into the barn, the flashlight beam sharp as a shout in the darkness, Sarah was not fully committed.

She knew it, she had known it in a carefully buried way ever since the plan to find the hidden diary had first entered her head. That was why her brain had supplied her with the thought of rats, the possibility that the flashlight might not be there or its batteries dead, the much likelier possibility that the Clemences would still be up, and notice and act upon a light moving about in the stable.

The flashlight hung from its accustomed hook; there was no sound of rats; the Clemence house was dark. Hunter had put the car in and closed the heavy sliding barn door; from the distance beyond the dully gleaming bulk of metal there was a faint feathery alarm from the quail and then the usual tapestried country quiet.

Sarah stood perfectly still, one hand on the latch of the door behind her, ready to re-open the way to security. (Or was it?) She was not brave by nature, and ridiculously sinister notions came to her constantly: what if she looked behind the chair where she was reading and a total stranger stood there, still as a statue, just staring at her? What if she came upon her stone marten scarf secretly chewing a morsel of meat in its narrow dark jaws? What if she went to meet a train and saw herself getting off and coming toward the car, or baby-sat for a friend and saw the tiny pink feet in the bassinet with their soles dirtied?

The night and the barn about her were real, but as yet untried. It was not like a high diving board, mounted in public view; she could lift the latch of the door and go back and no one would be the wiser. Any shame would be as private as the project itself.

It was a trick of light that made up her mind. When she moved the flashlight beam, it shot across the piled logs at the end of the barn. The open doorway into the stable, its wooden ramp hidden, turned into a tall black space like the one Charles had faced. Fatally weak, fatally trusting, plummeting through the bottomless night air.

She would always see that if she went back now. She would remember what all those people had managed to suggest to her, and she would think: Fifteen feet more, or twenty, and I could have proved they were wrong.

Or was the doubt hers, as much as the necessity?

Quiet in her flat slippers, shivering in the thin wool dress that had no collar or folds or loose sleeves to trammel her as she went in and out of the pens, Sarah advanced into the stable. Now that she had committed herself she didn't hesitate. She picked up the stick Milo had used to kill the mink, telling herself that she might have to pry up a plank, but comforted by the strong well-balanced weight of it. She located the Elliots with a sweep of the flashlight, roosting side by side in their nesting box, and unfastened the catch of the mesh door and went inside.

She stooped consciously, so as not to rise up to her full height and alarm them, but she needn't have worried; the Elliots, so active and distrustful by day, stared glassily ahead of them without stirring a feather. Perhaps they were terrified into immobility, or adopted it instinctively as a defensive measure. At any rate they didn't bother Sarah. She stirred the litter away from the planks with her slippered foot and probed at the corners with the stick. The planks were old but tight, and there were no new nail-heads and no stopped-up place to indicate the rat-hole that Peck had found and investigated.

Peck's death notice, because he had also found a diary?

The Silver had become alerted by the light and the sound of her progress; Sarah heard him grunt throatily and jump down, almost as heavily as a small child, from wherever he had been roosting. In the passing beam of the flashlight he faced her, magnificently black and white behind his crimson face. No one, he seemed to say, is going to bother *my* wife.

Sarah slipped into the Reeves' pen. The cock didn't like it; from an icy gold carving he sprang into a wild whir of wings, veering close to Sarah's bent face, veering back again. The hen, catching alarm from the beating feathers, shot madly around the enclosure, hit the wire, was stunned, and flew up again to a branch of the leaning bough. Sarah, who had lowered her head and not dared to look, proceeded by inches to the back of the pen.

Like the Elliots', the planks here were old and firm and untampered-with, at least as far as she could tell. The board partition met the flooring firmly, with no room for crevices. A long arch of barred tail-feather was within inches of her hand; the Reeves cock, however disturbed, could not prevent that in this enclosed place. Sarah moved respectfully around it, edged out of the pen, and fastened the door behind her.

She had somehow known it would be the Silvers: because they had been moved, because Charles had thought their pen innocent; most of all because of her own dread of them. Sarah stood motionless in the stable, the blackness about her deepened and thickened by the ringed disc of brilliance from the flashlight, the barn smell, at this moment, something she knew she would never forget. It was compounded of old timbers and litter and feed, hay and cement and leather, the whole brought alive by the indefinable scent of the birds. It wasn't a rank scent, or even musty; they were kept too scrupulously clean for that.

Was it possibly the smell of her own fear, or of anything done in darkness and secrecy?

Sarah could hear her heart and feel the moment when it accelerated slightly. Moving quietly, she crossed the cement floor and removed the lids of two metal containers before she found the one that held corn. What had Charles said the pheasants would do anything for? Raisins, or boiled potatoes. She hadn't seen any raisins on the kitchen shelves; she had an unstrung vision of herself going back inside and furtively boiling potatoes in the dark.

She would have to try the corn.

The Silver cock grunted as she approached the door of the pen, and the throaty sound rose and quickened almost to a honk as she opened it and stepped inside. The door closed behind her, and the cock came unhesitatingly forward; when Sarah released the stream of corn, he struck savagely at one kernel and then another, dashing them to one side. He stopped only when Sarah thrust the heavy stick toward him, at an angle across her own unprotected shins.

It stopped him. It also enraged him; his crest rose higher, and the crimson felt seemed to spread and engulf his furious face. He didn't back as she advanced with the stick; he dropped into a flanking position. Sarah moved the stick accordingly, turned her body slightly, shot the stream of the flashlight across the flooring of the pen.

At once, the light picked up a shiny point in the litter. Sarah bent for it unguardedly and felt lightning strike the outer end of her right eyebrow and flame down in an arc that was an outline of pain to come. It came, stinging savagely from the rake of a claw that had aimed for her eye, but in her hand she held the thing she had reached for.

A child's toy, one of a set of jacks.

"Those Elwell children," Bess had said about Long John's increasing viciousness. "They're absolute devils."

A child might have poked a long stick through the mesh in search of the jack, and excited the Silver's wrath. But—the flashlight enveloped the cock fully now—a child would not have been up late enough, nor been marksman enough, to open the wound just above the Silver's spur. Blood still flowed from it, cloaking one rosy leg in a fresh vivid red. It explained the Silver's excitability when he should have been roosting, and his instant attack upon Sarah.

It had been done—the knowledge was queerly slow in seeping through—not very long ago, to judge by all that bleeding. Unless it was a tremendously deep cut, or this was a haemophiliac pheasant, the wound had been inflicted quite recently. Not above a few minutes ago.

How long had she herself stood in the doorway of the barn, knowing that her committal would be complete; how long had it taken her to progress cautiously through the other two pens?

There was someone in the stable with her, as certainly as there had been someone in the room with her on the night of her arrival here. Breath held, body flattened into shadow, attention pinpointed. Brain groping after hers—no, jumping ahead of hers to this ultimate point.

A weight in her chest told Sarah that she had stopped breathing herself. She could not move naturally under this new and certain awareness; she straightened and stared uselessly into the blackness beyond the lip of light. She had been observed all the way—that was what had drummed the atmosphere of the barn into every pore—and her very presence in this pen was damning.

A great deal seemed to depend on pretending not to know she was watched. Her face hot with effort, her body stiff with it, Sarah held the stick mechanically in front of Long John and conducted the search she knew would be unavailing.

She found the open space toward the back of the pen, where the partition met the floor. It had begun as a rat-hole evidently, and in order to stop the tunnel at the source a foot-long strip of planking had been cut and lifted. The plank was not quite back in place. A line of shadow showed its tilt, and there was a sprinkle of decayed wood where the litter had been displaced.

There was no sound at all in the stable. The Silver cock had stopped his menacing grunts and stood at the opposite side of the pen, head thrust watchfully forward, ready to attack at the first opening. Not a feather stirred anywhere, nor a wisp of hay. It was an abnormal silence, as though the fierce concentration of someone standing—where? in the far corner near the medicine chest?—controlled even the two hundred year-old timbers of the barn.

Sarah's terror was baseless, she knew it even then. She could not be explained away like Nina Trafton, or Peck, or Charles, and as she wasn't going to find anything at all under the loose plank she didn't represent any real threat to whoever had killed them. But it was cold comfort. It did nothing to slow the alarming pace of her heart, the rapid thumpings that threatened to run together into one destroying thunder-clap thump.

To stand so close to the hands that had pushed Nina's head against the faucet, thrust Charles through a high window, sent Peck over the bridge and into the brook, battered at Miss Braceway's dead face—

Sanity as well as safety lay in playing out the rest of this useless game. She could not pretend that she was not suspicious, but she could appear balked and baffled. Sarah knew enough not to bend again before the Silver's eager amber-eyed stare. With the end of the stick and then the toe of her slipper, she tilted the loose section of plank out of place and shone the flashlight into the space beneath.

Something had lain here very recently, something edible, like leather-bound paper: the crumbled wood and soil wore a surface of blind white questing heads. Sarah saw them without a shudder; she had gone well past the stage of being horrified by worms. She nudged the plank back into position again, and it settled with a dull woody echo that sent the Silver cock flashing forward. Sarah was not quick enough with the stick; his beak stabbed into the calf of her left leg.

Queerly, she didn't dare to speak or even gasp at the surprising pain. It was as if any sound at all from her would disturb the infinitely delicate balance of the waiting darkness outside the pen. She had to go carefully toward the mesh door, because the Silver, triumphant at having put her to flight, grew bolder at every step. Her calf burned above a crawling trickle of blood, and at a sudden brand-new awareness of something she hadn't realized before, the deep curving scratch on her face began to blaze.

If the Silver's wound was as recent as she thought, if her presence with a flashlight had trapped X here, then the diary was here, too.

Her fingers shook over the fastening of the door, but that would be put down to the awkward grip of flashlight and stick, and not the fact that she had to turn her back briefly on that black and soundless corner.

But all at once the spell broke. Wood creaked in a slow, drawn-out secrecy; cold air came drenching over Sarah's feverish face. Someone said her name in a whisper, and said it again aloud. For Sarah it was like a stone thrown at glass, a match held to tinder: it destroyed her in a twinkling. She ran without control, stumbling up the wooden ramp into the barn, crying without knowing it, the flashlight beaconing crazily about her.

If she hadn't tripped, and gripped at the car fender to keep from sprawling, Harry Brendan would not have caught her there.

XVII

"SARAH! OH GOD, are you all right? *Sarah!*"

Sarah, still locked in a peculiar horror, flinched at the sound of her name rolling and echoing around the barn, just as her muscles had gone frantically rigid under the grip of Harry's hand. The rocketing flashlight beam had showed him coatless and tieless, his face wearing the jarred look of someone just waked.

Later, she could analyze her tongue-tied dread as the instinctive care people showed in the presence of a deadly snake. At the moment, all she could do was nod dumbly at Harry, push her tumbled hair back from her face, try to control her trembling and her heaving breath.

Harry took the flashlight from her and looked at her in its beam. "You're not all right," he said violently. "Who did that? Who's out there?"

He lifted his head at the growing sound of voices in the passageway. Sarah became simultaneously aware of two things: a distant barking of dogs, and a draught of cold air from the stable. How long had that been going on?

The barn was flooded suddenly with light. The blue door

opened and Bess Gideon, at the head of what seemed to be a small procession, blinked at them and said with the poise she carried even in the small hours of the morning, "Sarah—Harry. What is all this?"

Harry had encountered a protruding nail somewhere, he was rubbing absently at a long scratch on the inside of one wrist. He said pleasantly, "Bess, when I find out I will certainly let you know," and Sarah realized that with his first anxiety gone he was bitterly angry at her for not having confided in him, for attempting this on her own.

Faces turned toward Sarah and then away as just outside the stable door Rob Clemence's voice said irritably, "Nonsense, there's no smoke," and a moment later he and Kate came up the ramp and into the barn. His sardonic gaze examined the assembly; he said dryly, "I see. It's a come-as-you-are party, and Sarah and Harry have cheated."

. . . By their robes you shall know them, Sarah thought in a savingly unreal way. She could have identified each on its hanger: Bess's brusquely sashed navy blue, Hunter's austere Black Watch plaid, Milo's glittering foulard, Evelyn's quilted, ruffle-swamped peignoir. Kate wore beautifully tailored rose-red wool, Rob seemed to be poking fun at himself in regulation blue and gray and white stripes.

All present and accounted for. Which of them had had to make a run for it? Which pair of slippers wore, even after a rapid trip over cleansing grass, traces of the litter that clung to Sarah's? There hadn't been time to change slippers. One of them, even now, must be disciplining his lungs in order not to pant.

Milo said, "The secretary will now read the minutes of the last meeting," and the incongruity of the setting came sharply home—the barn floor puddled with sallow light, the vast shadowy loft above, the push of the wind, with occasional slicing success, at the cobwebby windows and the big door. Bess's poise surmounted even this. Hair wilder than usual, breath coming out in little gray puffs on the icy air, she said concernedly to Sarah, "You've hurt your face. What is all this, what's happened?"

I was awake, and I thought I heard a noise in the barn, said Sarah soundlessly inside her head, and I thought maybe a mink was after the pheasants and I could frighten him away. But I dropped the flashlight and it went out, and like a fool I went crashing around after it and fell against the woodpile.

She could say that, and dispel the feeling of naked danger that hung about her like a brilliant spotlight. She had proved to herself that Charles's death had been a contrived thing, not involving her, and she could take that comfort with her to the train. Harry Brendan would know she was lying, and one other person, but Harry knew his way to her apartment if he cared to find it and she would never see any of the rest of them again.

And Nina Trafton's diary—not in a deep bathrobe pocket, that would be too risky, nor even in the stable—could be retrieved and destroyed at leisure. Charles would not be avenged, but she had never undertaken that. She had only . . .

Rob Clemence had said it, and Harry; she had even said it to herself. She had only wanted to get out from under.

"I came to look for Nina's diary but I was too late," said Sarah, and although all their voices were altered in this big vaulted place, her own sounded unnecessarily loud and shocking. "The diary she really kept, the one whoever killed her took away and hid."

What followed had a dream-like quality, although it might have been the pounding of her blood in her ears that removed the scene a little for Sarah. But it was usually in dreams that people stood about robed and pajamaed in a great dim barn, oblivious of the cold, and discussed the dreamer as though she weren't there.

After the first blank wheeling of faces, and the outrage that came with realization of what Sarah had said, individual voices broke through and were chopped off by other voices. "Bess, are you going to stand there and—?" ". . . delayed reaction, that's all. People won't accept suicide, especially when—" "Didn't anybody tell her about Nina?"

Sarah didn't bother to separate the voices. She had braced herself against the cold for so long that there was a dull ache between her shoulder blades, and a deeper sharper ache until Harry Brendan broke his punishing silence. "There wasn't any suicide," he said in a short, hard voice. "Charles was pushed out of a window because he found out what Sarah just told you. Nina was killed, and Miss Braceway made the fatal mistake of trying to prove it, too."

On the far side of the barn the quail fluttered as blindly as moths, in a self-destructive rhythm that plucked badly at Sarah's nerves. Hunter said in a low bothered voice, "Harry, if all this is coming up, don't forget that Charles—"

"—prepared the way. Yes," said Harry. "He put a sedative in Miss Braceway's tea, enough to keep her out of the way so that he could have it out with Nina. But he didn't kill Nina and he didn't kill Miss Braceway, so it follows that he didn't kill himself in a handy fit of remorse."

Sarah glanced involuntarily at Kate Clemence. The luminous gray eyes were wide, the pale handsome lips set—and that was all.

Rob Clemence said harshly, "It seems to me we're throwing Nina's name around pretty freely."

Well, she had been his cousin, after all.

"Why?" said Evelyn suddenly and apologetically. "I mean why all this—why kill Nina in the first place?"

A swarm of answers seemed to fill the air like gnats. Because she was in a position of authority over the previous ruler of the farm, because she was intolerably pretty and efficient, because she was an unfaithful wife, because, used to the attentions of men, she might have scorned one man who couldn't take scorning, or, more probably, laughed at a man who couldn't take ridicule.

Milo shivered elaborately. He said mildly, "If anybody has two sticks I'll make a small fire," and nobody looked at him. Attention focussed on Bess, who had walked closer to Sarah with an air of decision.

"What do you mean, you were too late? Where was this—diary?"

"In the Silvers' pen," said Sarah, returning her gaze steadily. She put a finger to the searing scratch that curved out and down from her eyebrow. Only a faint smear of blood came away, it was almost dried. "You might look at Long John's leg. It was bleeding pretty badly a few minutes ago."

Bess might have stayed all night in the barn, crisply and courteously discussing the question of Nina's problematical diary; mention of an injury to one of her birds sent her striding off to the stable at once, robe switching agitatedly around her ankles. The light went on there, followed by the metallic sound of the mesh door opening and the anxious croon of Bess's voice.

Rob Clemence studied Sarah with his tufty eyebrows up. "Long John gave as good as he got, didn't he?"

"I didn't touch him," Sarah said coldly, and gradually, stealthily, glances began to slide around. They noted the long scratch on Harry Brendan's arm, the marks on Sarah's face and leg; they were balked everywhere else by robes and pajamas and even, on Evelyn's hands, the little cream-lined gloves she wore at night.

Something close to an answer shot through Sarah's mind, and was blanked out by Kate's cool deliberate voice. "How do you know there was another diary, Sarah? How do you know where it was? Forgive me if I say that I can't believe Charles told you."

Evelyn sucked in a breath of excitement, loud in the wind-brushed silence. Beside Sarah, so close that their shoulders touched, Harry drew in a slower and more dangerous breath. He liked Kate, and he had an old loyalty to her as he had to all these people, but with the peculiar inter-knowledge that had always existed between them Sarah knew that he was about to say something unforgivable.

She said lightly, "That's asking quite a lot, isn't it, Kate?" and then, because it wasn't entirely a lie, "Charles did tell me."

The white face, beautifully chiselled under the carelessly cropped dark hair, turned involuntarily as though a blow had landed. Sarah tried to feel sorry and could not. Hunter said frowningly, "If you're going by a diary—well, nobody goes unscathed in a diary, does he? That's what they're for."

And suppose, thought Sarah suddenly, that that was exactly why the diary had been kept? If it showed Nina involved in one or more extra-marital affairs, and if she had been killed for a different reason, wouldn't the diary be the perfect safeguard in case an investigation were pressed? It would point to this man or that; it would obscure any other issue.

A man had certainly gone to Dr. Vollmer, presenting himself as Charles Trafton, laying the foundation for Charles's death. But suppose he hadn't known that at the time, suppose it had been put to him that it was only a necessary measure to discredit anything Charles might say?

Hunter would have done it for Bess, Rob for Kate. In spite of the automatic mockery which he intended for wit, Milo might even have done it for Evelyn.

And what was it that had offered itself to Sarah's brain before Kate dispelled it?

Bess called from the stable, her voice so controlled that the anger behind it was clear. She was already leather-gloved, she wanted Kate to bring the antiseptic from the wall cabinet. She looked taller and higher-headed than usual, coming back into the barn moments later. Her face was dangerously flushed.

She said in a clipped voice, "You say you didn't touch him, Sarah?"

"No. I held him off with the stick. He flew at me," said Sarah, "when I went to pick up this."

She had been holding the jack in her clenched hand, completely unaware of it all this time. When she extended her palm, everybody moved forward to look. The jack was obviously new and unplayed-with, its points glittering. Milo said with an air of triumph, "There you are, those Elwell kids. Why aren't they in a pen, by the way?"

"The Elwells and their children left for California on Thursday," said Bess distinctly, "and I changed the litter in the Silvers' pen this morning—yesterday morning."

Milo wouldn't have known; he had been at the dentist's.

Or had someone else used that as a double bluff? Sarah's head ached with tension and the effort of trying to remember some small and very significant thing.

The wind blew through crevices in the barn, the quail bounded, and nobody stirred, nobody said, "Let's go in."

"Someone," Bess was saying in that ominously clamped-down voice, "nearly broke Long John's leg. The spur is broken as it is; it won't heal normally." At Milo's surreptitious, "Is that bad?" she wheeled; she said in a cutting voice Sarah had never heard from her before, "Milo, you're a little old for clowning. Sarah, didn't you get a glimpse of anyone in the stable?"

Had she ever said there was someone in the stable with her? Sarah said, "No," and knew that the brief pause had been dangerous in the extreme. She had shone the flashlight at random when she first entered the stable. How was X to be sure that it had not touched the tips of a pair of motionless slippers, a fold of foulard or plaid or stripes or quilting, or a flicker of rose-red?

But not Kate, surely, who had loved Charles, who had been engaged to him and then, after Nina Trafton's appearance on the scene, unengaged. She might have hated Nina for that, but she would never have placed Charles in jeopardy, nor killed him.

Foulard or plaid, stripes or quilting or rose-red—the barrier in Sarah's mind came tumbling down. Why had she never seen this before, the one thing that ran consistently through it all? The tale told to the psychiatrist, the tiny thread of fabric under Charles's fingernail after his death, the rifling of Bess's travelling case on the night of Sarah's arrival, the smear of paint on Milo's portrait of Nina.

Was it possible that no one else knew? But it was so elemental that it might be passed by as a personal vagary, of no importance. Sarah could take Bess aside and ask her, but could she even trust Bess, whose whole existence lay in the farm, who bore the Silver pheasant's mark between thumb and forefinger?

Harry Brendan's hand drifted to Sarah's, touched it secretly, held it tightly. Sarah's head swam a little at the private contact; it seemed, at this moment, much more piercing than a kiss. She couldn't find a safe pair of eyes, so she gazed beyond the others into the stable, still lighted, as she said, "I didn't see anybody in the stable, but I know where it all started. As far as I'm concerned, I mean. The psychiatrist said Charles had nightmares about me, about a walk we took together here just before we were married."

The narrowing of attention was almost an atmospheric thing, like a sharp drop in the barometer, a promise of thunder. Sarah had to transfer her gaze to the woodpile, because Bess—deliberately?—had not fastened the door of the Silvers' pen. It hung open a good four inches, and the Silver cock, whose furious grunting had become a part of the background, was just about to find it out.

XVIII

"CHARLES AND I went through the woods and up to the bluff," Sarah said. (If only someone would stop the quail's soft, senseless, ceaseless battering off in the ragged shadows.) She looked at Evelyn, and the full blue gaze met hers and swelled with interest. "A woman had come, with her children . . ."

"Jane Folsom," said Evelyn promptly. Her lashes were busy. "She stayed forever, and the children were ghastly. I didn't blame you and Charles for sneaking off."

"I had a scarf in my pocket, and I started to put it on when it got windy. It blew into Charles's face just as he reached the edge of the bluff. It was only a little bit of silk," said Sarah steadily, "but it might have made him go over the edge, I suppose."

A plank creaked hollowly as someone's weight shifted. The very corner of Sarah's eye saw the Silver cock, crimson face thrusting, test the door of his pen, find it open, come jumping out. He stood erect in a position of triumph and menace, great wings beating, and although the wind around the barn covered the rapid clicking sound, Sarah suspected that none of them would have heard it anyway. The tight attention of one had spread to them all.

"What someone told the psychiatrist in New York was that Charles believed I wanted him to fall, and that it got to be an obsession with him, to the point where he was terrified of me."

Kate Clemence's face had the closed unyielding look of statuary; Bess was rigidly intent; Evelyn's skin was patched with red. Milo had taken off his glasses and was polishing them on a fold of his robe, as though fearful of missing a single detail; Rob Clemence, hands thrust tensely into his pockets, waited with an expression of incredulity.

The Silver cock came stalking up the ramp.

Hunter's shadowed face moved forward into the light, so bent upon Sarah that they might have been alone in the barn. "Then somebody was obviously out of his mind. As I remember it, the two of you came back holding hands, which isn't the usual manifestation of terror."

Don't look at the Silver, head furiously down and forward, rose-pink feet, one blood-darkened, quickening as he came closer to the attacker with the slashing stick. "That might have been another day," said Sarah carefully. "I think I came back first, as a matter of fact."

"No, you were together. Charles was wearing the old tweed coat he kept here, and you had on a raincoat and a blue scarf."

Oddly, it was a wrench—until she remembered what he had done to Charles, what he had so casually tried to do to her. "It wasn't blue," said Sarah, staring at him across three feet of tingling space, "it was green. You saw it the other day when you got my raincoat out of the closet, and you still thought it was blue. You're colorblind, aren't you, Hunter?

That's why you got mixed up between my suitcase and Bess's the first night I was here and you came for the train ticket, that's why you put that blob of green paint on the background of Milo's portrait. Did you—" her voice broke without warning "—*hold* the blue curtain out to Charles as he was going over the—over the—"

Evelyn screamed and ran scuttlingly; she gasped over her shoulder, "Bess, the Silver's out!"

Long John came steadily forward. He was of a bad-tempered breed at best, and age had not improved his disposition. The pain of his broken spur, the memory of having been slashed at in an enclosed place, had wiped out any hesitation before the light and the collection of legs and faces. He had been cunningly silent when he commenced his stalk—now he was uttering his peculiar challenge, half-cry, half-grunt.

Rob stepped back, and jerked Kate with him. Bess stood with the rigidity of iron; so did Hunter although he looked suddenly ill. Evelyn was crouched in the far corner of the barn; Sarah turned in the hard circle of Harry Brendan's arm and saw the Silver's powerful snowy wings stretch to an incredible span.

"Bess," said Milo in a mounting voice, "get this damned bird—"

"No," said Bess in a voice as still and unflinching as her pose, and the Silver launched himself at Milo.

It was a frightful thing to watch. Deprived of the stick, of any weapon at all, Milo was caught in a primitive terror of the beating wings, the seeking claws, the furious beak. He ran blindly across the barn, and the Silver, infected by frenzy, plummeted at his back. Blood from the reopened wound made a streak of red on the foulard, more vivid than dye, and drove the cock to fresh fury.

Milo held an arm across his eyes, but he did not cry out again. It was Harry Brendan who said tensely, "Oh my God," and walked across the barn fast and snatched the long-handled, metal-rimmed net from its position on the wall. As the Silver flew at Milo's shining, maddeningly glassed-in eyes, he flung the net. It fell with a clatter, striking one snowy black-veined feather, but it did not deflect the Silver for an instant; if anything it accentuated his rage. The crimson face turned only glancingly, the coarse brilliantly black crest seemed to stand even more erect. Harry threw the net again, and the cock launched himself into a strong web of nylon.

There was silence, and then a thrashing and a sound of breaking feathers. Cut in two places, Sarah nevertheless turned away; she could not bear to look at the beautiful vicious strength tattering itself inside the net.

Milo patted his pocket for a handkerchief, found none, and wiped his face with his sleeve. He said pantingly to Bess, "You won't—have him long—I promise you. There was sleeping sickness—last year—and pheasants are carriers—and this is the end of yours."

"Where is the diary?" said Bess. She would, thought Sarah with distant amazement, have been just as stony with Hunter. For all her poses—her battered clothes by day, her stark elegant black after six—she was a woman without compromise in any direction.

"You know," said Milo, fumbling at his glasses, sliding them down in a painful parody of his old mocking way, "that diary is better unfound. You don't show up in it terribly well, Bess, and Edward's made a total fool of. Charles looks like an idiot, but a dangerous one. Harry had his eye on her, and Hunter used to meet her out in the hut—"

"To go digging ferns. Edward thought she found them by herself," said Hunter, but he had flushed darkly, as though at the realization of Nina's secret amusement. "God . . . *I* told you about that business on the bluff, because I said we ought to have the woods posted in case children should wander in . . ."

Long John crouched quietly in the net, guarding his plumage. Bess, her face bitter, put on her leather gloves and bent swiftly, pinning the strong wings and picking up the netted bundle so that the metal handle trailed on the barn floor. She said quietly, "Do you know, I've half a mind to let him out again," and for a nightmarish second it seemed possible that she would.

Harry Brendan said between his teeth, "You're being too modest, Milo. Surely you crop up somewhere in the diary? What does Nina have to say about you?"

Milo's face glittered, otherwise he might not have heard. He said in a voice that went high with triumph, "She wasn't Rob's cousin at all. Oh, far from it. She was his—"

Given a chalk, thought Sarah, he would have enjoyed writing obscenities on walls. Something, Rob's step forward or the fact that Bess still held the Silver cock and had turned, stopped him.

"Old flame," said Bess with an urbanity that gave Sarah a wild impulse to laughter. The impulse died when the very tail of her eye caught the look of total shock on Kate Clemence's face. Obviously Kate had accepted the tale of cousinship, and had put Nina Trafton down as a necessary evil when Charles was so innocently dazzled by her. And that, of course, was the reason behind Rob's hostility toward Sarah and any investigation of Nina. Kate was not going to forgive him easily or quickly for having introduced the woman who was, in a sense, the cause of Charles's destruction.

"Nina had only enough money for her fare east," Bess was saying coolly, "and Rob was the only person who could give her introductions here. It was all quite a long time ago in any case. Did you really think you had something to hold over Nina's head, Milo? She told me about it herself. And I really don't think I care to learn why you wanted something to hold over her head, or what went on between you at all. I have a feeling that it would be rather disgusting."

On that she walked off to the stable, her straight back full of distaste, her dignity enhanced, if anything, by the flapping robe and trailing handle of the net. Her voice came back to them soothingly—"There, Long John. There, boy," —and Sarah's sense of reality slipped another notch. There was still a lot left of the night, and because a pheasant could not give evidence to the police they would all go back to bed, presently, and wait for the darkness to blow itself away just as though the same roof did not harbor this owlish, head-tipping, murderous man. In spite of everything that had been said and done in the cold echoing barn, the hand-hewn timbers would merely swallow another secret, because there wasn't a shred of proof. All Milo had to do was deny everything.

But of course they wouldn't go to bed, and it would not be quite that simple for Milo. They would get dressed and look for and find the diary, and it would carry Milo's fingerprints. In the morning Sarah would call Lieutenant—Welk, was it? It seemed so long ago—and Dr. Vollmer, and when

Vollmer had identified Milo as the man who had come to him under the name of Charles Trafton, what had been suicide would be re-investigated as murder. And when you held two ends of a string, you could work away little by little at the knots in between.

Milo turned abruptly toward the passage door. Although he was shivering from the contact of cold air on sweat, he said with a faint and dreadful jauntiness, "Well, *I'm* not crazy, and I'm going to bed. Evelyn?"

They had all forgotten Evelyn, still crouched in the corner where she had fled at the sight of the Silver cock. She came forward now with a look of docile obedience, and when she was two feet away from Milo she said with total detachment, "I know why he killed her."

And this was what Evelyn had waited for, this was the diamond-sharpness that had peeped out now and then from behind the bumbling and fumbling and inanity. She had borne Milo's mechanical taunts almost with pleasure, adding them to the limitless price he would pay when he was caught and punished, and it was somehow typical of her that she would do nothing herself but wait for it to come through an outside agency, with a kind of terrible patience.

Milo's incredulity touched his face like a spasm and was gone. Evelyn said calmly, "She found that letter of yours, about buying that strip of land when you'd always told Bess the owner refused to sell, and she got curious about where you were getting the money from. She found that out, too, and she told you she'd tell Bess you'd been doctoring tax returns and stealing from the farm for years if you didn't leave her alone. But you didn't kill her for that; you killed her for laughing at you when you thought you could have a cozy little affair with her. I heard her. She said if you'd only feather out a little m-more," Evelyn's voice stumbled at last, tears began to slip from the edges of her eyelids in a mixture of hysteria and hatred and some old remnant of love, "you'd remind her of a g-great spectacled sapsucker."

No one smiled, no one stirred.

"And you said," went on the trembling voice, "'Funny, aren't you? Better watch out you don't kill yourself laughing.' Sarah, somebody, get me *out of here* . . ."

The diary wasn't hard to find, once the stable itself had been eliminated. In order to have reappeared as quickly as he had, Milo could only have slipped out the stable door into the corral, rounded the barn, streaked across the lawn and entered the house by the front door. Surprised at the foot of the stairs by Bess, he had told her that he too had been roused by the barking of the mink farm Dobermans, always a signal of alarm in the country. And there were barberry bushes in the angle between stable and barn, and a thick clump of rhododendrons at the corral entrance. . . .

It was a dreadful, flashlight-prowling night that Sarah would remember as long as she lived, although in her exhaustion it went by her in splashes, like street-lamps on an immensely long black journey.

She sat with Evelyn who talked incessantly in spite of the sedative Bess had given her. Evelyn had kept a mental record of every damning scrap of information that could be used against Milo, shoring up conjecture with her own shrewd analysis of Milo's reactions as well as with the answers she got from Sarah and the others. The police would find witnesses, break alibis, trap Milo in a web of circumstantial evidence, but their indictment would not be more complete.

Evelyn went back to the day of Nina's death when she

had watched Milo follow Charles from the gamebird show. It would have been easy for Milo to wait unobserved until Charles had left the farmhouse, to take advantage of Miss Braceway's drugged sleep to push Nina's head down in the washbasin, holding it there while she died. Hiding Nina's diary in the pheasant pen, Milo had slipped back into the crowd at the game show. He was, said Evelyn grimly, as shocked and incredulous as everyone else when Nina's death was discovered on their return home. He must have congratulated himself on a perfect murder until Miss Braceway's stubborn probing began to arouse curiosity. Her fatal rendezvous with Milo at the hut on the mink farm put an end to that danger.

After Peck's release as a suspect for the nurse's murder, Milo realized Charles would have to be silenced, too. He may have overheard Charles talking about his guilt to Harry. It was just as likely that Milo's instinct for self-preservation helped him to make a correct diagnosis of Charles's moodiness. He knew too much about Charles's involvement in Nina's death to accept Kate's theory that Charles was brooding over his recklessly unsuitable marriage. It was easy for Milo to arrange to run into Charles in New York, to maneuver the conversation so that Charles, who was close to the breaking point, would admit his decision to reveal his part in Nina's death in the hope that her murderer would be found.

It was then that Charles must have told Milo that he had found the key to Nina's diary. Evelyn remembered that when they were all in New York for Charles's funeral Milo had gone into Sarah's bedroom. He took the framed snapshot of Charles to prevent Dr. Vollmer from seeing it, but he did not find the incriminating key, not even later on at the farmhouse when he ripped the lining of Bess's travelling case in a final vain search.

Unfortunately Milo had not taken the time to invite more confidences from Charles before he had sent him plunging from the apartment window. He did not know Charles had guessed the murderer had hidden the missing diary in a pheasant pen. It would have to be an indoor pen with plenty of hiding places, a pen occupied by birds militant enough to stand off an inquisitive meddler. Only a few hours before his death, Charles had listed the names of the ill-tempered Reeves and Elliots. Their pens would be the best to conceal the diary. He had scratched out the Silvers, not knowing that they had been moved indoors, that the diary could be guarded by the savage Long John.

If Milo had known about that very last entry in Charles's engagement book, he could have reclaimed the incriminating diary before Sarah, probing and prying and coming closer to the secret of Charles's death, had returned to the farm. There would not have had to be the hurried dangerous trip to the stables at night to get the diary, with the risk of injuring an attacking Long John. Milo had hoped that the jack he left in the pen would make Bess believe that the children had damaged the bird. Otherwise he had to trust to luck that his raid would be successful. He could not take the chance of Sarah finding the evidence that would link him to Nina's death and from there to the murder of the nurse and Charles and of Peck. Probably no one would ever discover if Peck had had real evidence for his blackmail, or if he had merely suspected Milo was guilty. Whichever it was, Peck was a security risk and therefore expendable.

Milo had seen everyone as a threat to his security—everyone but Evelyn. He had been too contemptuously sure of her stupidity to notice her hostile, unobtrusive spying on his every move. He had never guessed it was she who in a defiant challenge had painted a tiny pair of horn-rimmed glasses above and behind Nina in the portrait, glasses that Milo with forethought had painted out in green. He had thought himself safe from everybody but Sarah. . . .

Sarah's eyelids fell, the night lurched and steadied again. And here was the diary, supposition made real in the crumbled dark-blue leather and mouse-nibbled pages. Hunter, who had found it, handled it with grim care; after one glance Bess avoided it as though it were an asp.

Sleep must have caught her again, because Milo was suddenly there in the living room, emerged from his dangerous silence upstairs and so icily pale that his dark hair and horn-rimmed glasses were like something painted on a subway poster. He carried a suitcase in one of the soft plump hands that had killed four people, but he wore his air of challenge badly. The pounding pulse, the trapped fear, showed under it like a woman's hanging slip. He said to someone behind Bess in the dining room doorway, "I'll sue, you know. Slander, defamation of character, false arrest, the works."

"Officer," said Bess steadily—and Sarah had been asleep, and for some time, because there was a uniformed man at Bess's shoulder. "My nephew has been planning flight, for the reasons I've told you. I haven't missed any cash from the house, but there's a gold watch, an heirloom, that I haven't been able to find."

Milo's mouth curled. He submitted confidently to the policeman's embarrassed search; his jaw dropped blankly when Charles's gold watch was removed from his suit coat pocket. The policeman interrupted a spate of cursing to turn to Bess. "Well now, do you want to press charges, Mrs. Gideon? I mean . . . ?"

People never did, in families, they had it out among themselves. In spite of the weird tale he had been told, they would decide against the police blotter, the inevitable publicity in a small town.

"Yes," said Bess. She put her face into her hands, but only for a second. "Yes, I want to press charges, Officer."

The pheasants called shrilly in the dawn, their chopped-off shrieks as surprising on the air as their color was in the pearl and charcoal light. Sarah, walking about the pens for the last time, lifted her face now and then as though the wet and piercing cold were rain. She gave a final piece of bread to the bantam rooster, who stood back gallantly for his hens and never got a crumb, raisins to the Manchurians and the Amhersts, a shredded leaf of lettuce to the Japanese Coppers.

She could not bring herself to go near the Silvers.

Behind her the house was quiet, although only Evelyn slept. Hunter had accompanied Milo and the policeman, to turn over the diary which would have to be read and then, because of the respect accorded Bess in the town, treated with all possible discretion. The Clemences, shedding with their robes a little of the dream-like quality of the night, had returned to stay with Bess. It was as though a year had been wiped out and someone lay upstairs in danger of death.

Sarah emerged onto the back lawn. There was the cherry tree she had gazed at from the window of the attic room, and hanging from one of its lower branches the crow's cage, its door propped open. When the echo of the front door closing had roused the crow to say horrifyingly, "Hi, Milo," Bess's rigid poise had cracked apart; she had said in a trembling voice, "Hunter, will you please— I can't, I cannot stand . . ."

And now the crow was trying to make up its mind. It tipped its head in a dreadful mimicry, half arched its black wings, stooped to peer incredulously at the open door. Inside were food and water and security. Outside . . .

Footsteps came quietly across the cold gray grass. Sarah turned her head and said to Harry in a whisper, "Look," and they stood without speaking while the crow hopped off its perch, sidled to the door, and rolled a bright wary eye at these people who obviously didn't know what he was about to do. Sarah was prepared to clap her hands to her ears, but the crow only ruffled itself briefly and took off in a beating of wings, soaring over the far fields, disappearing in the woods.

"That's a smart crow," said Harry, his voice not quite his own. He stood scrupulously apart from her, because it was one thing to know each other instantly over a barrier, and a very different thing when the barrier was gone. His face was sober and thoughtful, thinner and older than when Sarah had first seen it, and infinitely dearer. "The car is ready. . . . Coming?"

Sarah had an advantage over the crow; she knew perfectly well, she had always known, what lay outside. "Coming," she said.